ALSO BY

DOMENICO STARNONE

First Execution

TIES

Domenico Starnone

TIES

Translated from the Italian
by Jhumpa Lahiri

Europa
editions

Europa Editions
214 West 29th Street
New York, N.Y. 10001
www.europaeditions.com
info@europaeditions.com

This book is a work of fiction. Any references to historical events,
real people, or real locales are used fictitiously.

Library of Congress Cataloging in Publication Data is available
ISBN 978-1-60945-385-5

Starnone, Domenico
Ties

Winner of the Inaugural edition of *The Bridge Prize* for Best Novel

Book design by Emanuele Ragnisco
www.mekkanografici.com

Cover illustration © Jonathan McHugh/Getty

Prepress by Grafica Punto Print – Rome

Printed in the USA

CONTENTS

TIES

INTRODUCTION
By Jhumpa Lahiri

T he need to contain and the need to set free: these are the contradictory impulses, the positive and negative charges that interact in Domenico Starnone's novel, *Ties*. To contain, in Italian, is *contenere*, from the Latin verb *continere*. It means to hold, but it also means to hold back, repress, limit, control. In English, too, we strive to contain our anger, our amusement, our curiosity.

A container is designed so that something can be placed inside it. It has a double identity in that it is either lacking contents or occupied: either empty or full. Containers often hold what is precious. They house our secrets. They keep us safe but can also imprison, ensnare. Ideally, containers stem chaos: they are supposed to keep things from dispersing, disappearing. *Ties* is a novel full of containers, both literal and symbolic. In spite of them, things go missing.

The characters in *Ties* are few: a family of four, a neighbor, a lover who remains offstage. A cat, a *carabiniere,* a couple of strangers. But there are a number of inanimate objects that also play critical roles in the alchemy of this novel: a swollen envelope that holds a bundle of letters, a hollow cube. Photographs, a dictionary, shoelaces, a home. And what do these objects represent, if not agents of enclosure of various kinds? Envelopes hold letters, and letters contain one's innermost thoughts. Photos contain time, a home contains a family. A hollow cube can contain whatever we'd like it to. A dictionary contains words. Laces—the literal translation of the Italian title, *Lacci*—serve to close up our shoes, which in turn contain our feet.

And as these objects are opened one by one—once the elastic around the envelope is removed, once laces are untied—the novel ignites. Like Pandora's box, each of these objects unleashes acute forms of suffering: frustration, humiliation, yearning, jealousy, envy, rage.

If the myth of Pandora is the leitmotif of *Ties*, Chinese boxes are the underlying mechanism, the morphology. The entire structure of this novel, in fact, seems to me a series of Chinese boxes, one element of the plot discretely and impeccably nestled within the next. There is no hole in the construction, no fissure. No detail has escaped the author's attention; like the home of Aldo and Vanda—the husband and wife at the center of this fleet tale—everything is in place, neat as a pin.

In spite of this airtight structure, the effect is exactly the opposite. A volcanic energy erupts, circulates, spills over in these pages. The novel reckons with messy, uncontrollable urges that threaten to break apart what we hold sacred. It is, in fact, about what happens when structures—social, familial, ideological, mental, physical—fall apart. It asks why we go out of our way to create structures if only to resent them, to evade them, to dismantle them in the end. It is about our collective, primordial need for order, and about our horror, just as primordial, of closed spaces.

Chinese boxes are of course an established narrative device to describe a story that is artfully contained within another story: examples include Lampedusa's short story "The Siren," Mary Shelley's *Frankenstein*. *Ties* plays whimsically with this conceit. It is one novel but it is also several. Though the elements are precisely aligned, though they correspond to one another, they are also severed. One can read the novel as three panels of a triptych, but the image of Chinese boxes remains in my opinion more apt, in that it suggests an infinite number of openings and closings, an endless game.

Let's take it a step further and regard the novel itself as a narrative container. I first called *Ties* a Pandora's box, and then a series of Chinese boxes, but it is also a magician's box that enchants us, from which things appear and disappear. The story jumps around, shifting tonally. And though I have just posited that it is an extremely orderly novel, it is also a gloriously messy one. Points of view are distinct but also blur, time leaps back and forth, expanding and contracting. The trajectory is point to point but also elliptical. The effect is coherent but unpredictable, blissfully free of norms.

Starnone's genius is his ability to play constantly both inside and outside the box, now conforming to it, now escaping it. It is this double-pronged illusion that gives the novel such equilibrium, such force. Though perfectly plotted, though utterly satisfying, this is a novel without a formal conclusion. We never see the end of it. There are obvious scenes to come, always more boxes to confront. The finale has been truncated and we are left in suspense. Only a writer with dexterity of the highest order is capable of pulling off a trick like this.

The metaphor of the magician's box leads us to one of the central, recurrent themes in *Ties*: that of being deceived, betrayed. Whether cheated by an anonymous hustler or an errant husband, by a trick of the mind or fortune's whims, characters are repeatedly being duped, hoodwinked, fooled, lied to. Adultery, in this novel, implies both a physical and moral transgression: stepping outside the family home, breaking the bond between husband and wife. Although breaking that bond may entail little more than moving from one enclosure to the next.

In spite of all the solid walls, the reassuring structures we seek out and build around us, there is nowhere, Starnone seems to suggest, to feel safe. Life is what betrays the container, what spills out. Cesare Pavese comes to mind; in his short story "Suicidi" (Suicides) he observes, "La vita è tutto un tradimento"—*All of life is betrayal*. That is to say, time betrays us, people we know and don't know betray us, we betray ourselves by living, by growing old, and, finally, by dying. Starnone complicates Pavese's observation—unpacking it, if you will. *Ties* is less about betrayal than about pain that returns, that resurfaces: in spite of diligent efforts to organize experiences, emotions, memories, they can't be packaged, hidden, repressed, filed away. Fittingly, at one point, there is a dream in these pages—a fecund, indelible image. For dreams both contain and set free the roiling matter of our psyches.

The multiple themes encased in the novel are densely layered. It is a rumination on old age, on the passage of time, on frailty, on solitude. On forms of inheritance: economic, genetic, emotional. It is a book about marriage, about procreation, about parenting, about love. Love is a key word in *Ties*, a term that is questioned, redefined, shunned, treasured, maligned. At one point Vanda says that love is merely "a container we stick everything into." It is, in essence, a hollow vessel, a placeholder that justifies our behaviors and choices. A notion that consoles us, that cons us more often than not.

In spite of its stormy course, its dark vision, *Ties* points faithfully toward freedom and its corollary, happiness. Be they virtues or privileges, be they considered a crime, freedom and happiness, in this novel, are one and the same: wild states of being that refuse to be domesticated, that cannot be trammeled or curbed. *Ties* looks coldly at the price of freedom and happiness. It both celebrates and castigates Dionysian states of ecstasy, of abandon. And though happiness often involves linking ourselves to other people—in other words, stepping outside the confines of ourselves—it is something, in the final analysis, that characters experience privately, alone.

Pandora's box sets free the evils of the world. Only hope

remains. *Ties,* too, though caustic, though troubling, remains a hopeful novel. It is bathed in light, it contains moments of great tenderness. It is lyrical, agile, energetic. It is also very funny. It is a great work of literature. And nothing gives me more hope than this.

As the translator of *Ties* into English, I too have had to break open a formidable container: the container of Italian. For many years I have searched within that box, trying to piece together a new sense of myself. My relationship to Italian incubates and evolves in a sacred vessel I hold dear. My impulse has been to guard it, to not contaminate it.

Then I read *Ties* when it was published in Italy, in the autumn of 2014, and fell in love with it. I had not yet translated anything from Italian to English. In fact, I was resistant to the idea. I was immersed in Italian, in a joyous state of self-exile from the language (English) and the country (the United States) that have marked me most significantly. But the impact of this novel overwhelmed me and my desire, as soon as I read it, was to translate it someday.

I identified strongly with Aldo because, like him, I had run away, in my case to Italy, taking refuge in the Italian language in search of freedom and happiness. I found them there. Then, like Aldo, after some euphoric years away, with certain misgivings, I decided to return. I moved back to the city that had once been home, where I was surrounded by the language I had deliberately stepped away from. I did all this with a broken heart.

The month after I returned to the United States, *Ties* won the Bridge Prize for fiction, awarded each year to a contemporary Italian novel or story collection that will be translated into English, and to an American work of fiction that will be translated into Italian. I read the novel for a second time, even more moved by it, and then I discussed it with the author at a panel at the Italian Embassy in Washington, D.C. Following the event, Starnone asked if I would consider translating it. I said yes. As a result, this novel has accompanied me during a particularly challenging year of my life. Incidentally, much of it was translated as I was packing up my home, putting everything I have accumulated in my life into a series of boxes.

As a translator I remain outside the container, in that the novel remains the brainchild of a fellow writer. It is liberating in that I don't have to fabricate anything. But I am bound to a preexisting text, and thus aware of a greater sense of responsibility. There is nothing to invent but everything to get right. There is the challenge of transplanting into a different language what already thrives, beautifully, in another. In order to translate *Ties* I had to purposefully distance myself from Italian, the language I have come to love most, dismantling it, rendering it invisible.

In Starnone's novel, life has to be reread in order to be fully experienced. Only when things are reread, reexamined, revisited, are they understood: letters, photos, words in dictionaries. Translation, too, is a processing of going back over things again and again, of scavenging and intuiting the meaning, in this case multivalent, of a text. The more I read this novel, the more I discovered.

I was struck, as I translated, by a fertile lexicon of terms that mean or describe a state of disorder. I made a list of them: *a soqquadro, devastazione, caos, disordine. Sfasciato, squinternato, divelto, sfregiato. Scempio, disastro, buttare per aria.* These terms are stemmed by a single, prevailing, recurrent word: *ordine.* Order. Or perhaps it is order that is constantly under threat, the terms for disaster engulfing it, undermining it.

Another word that stood out to me, that is used frequently, is *scontento.* It can mean unhappiness in English, but it is far stronger than that. It is an amalgam of frustration, dissatisfaction, disappointment, discontent. And though the roots are different, I couldn't help but ponder the proximity, the interplay between certain verbs in the Italian that sound or look similar, that are the-matically linked: *contenere* (to contain) and *contentare* (to make happy). *Allacciare* (to lace, tie down) and *lasciare* (to leave). As I've already noted, the title of this novel, in Italian, is *Lacci*, which means shoelaces. We see them on the cover, thanks to an illustration chosen by the author himself. A per-son, presumably a man, wears a pair of shoes whose laces are tied together. It is a knot that will surely trip him up, that will get him nowhere. We don't see the expression on the man's face, in fact we see very little of his body. And yet we fear for him, feel a little sorry for him, perhaps laugh at him, given that he already seems to be in the act of falling on his face.

But *lacci* in Italian are also a means of bridling, of capturing something. They connote both an amorous link and a restrain-ing device. "Ties" in English straddles these plural meanings. "Laces" would not have. Having made this choice, I am struck by the relationship in English, too, between *untie* and *unite,* two opposing actions counterpoised in this novel.

What happens when laces are untied? Indeed, as I have already argued, the entire novel is a series of tying and untying, of putting in order and pulling apart, of creating and destroy-ing. "Writing is more about destroying than creating," Karl Ove Knausgård has observed. There is some truth to this. But art is nothing if not contained by a unique structure, held in place by an inviolable unique form.

My American friend and fellow translator from Italian, Michael Moore, believes that Starnone—a Neapolitan writer who grew up speaking dialect, who learned to write in Italian, as so many Italian writers do—is one of the few contemporary Italian authors today who writes in an uncontaminated Italian. My Italian writer friends, too, hail his transparent, nuanced, eru-dite prose. I agree with them. Its rhythm, its lexicon floats free from any trend. His style is protean. His sentences can be lap-idary but others are intricate, centripital, revealing a subtle inlay of clauses—Chinese boxes on the syntactical level. In translating them I have often had to rupture their design, restructuring in order to render them at home in English. His prose is steeped in classical allusions, psychoanalytic references, the laws of physics.

This novel, his thirteenth work of fiction, fits into no distinct category or genre: it is a clever whodunit, a comedy of errors, a domestic drama, a tragedy. It is an astute commentary on the sexual revolution, on women's liberation, on rational and irrational urges. It is like a cube, perfectly proportioned; turn it around, and you will discover another facet.

There is a passage in this novel that stopped me in my tracks the first time I encountered it, that moves me in particular each time I reread it. It involves a writer alone in his study, not writing but, rather, sorting through his books and papers. It is a meditation on existence and on identity in its most essential form, and it helps me to understand the impetus behind what I myself do. It is a passage about leaving traces, about trying desperately, in vain, to tie ourselves to life itself. It lays bare the flawed human impulse to endure.

Writing is a way to salvage life, to give it form and meaning. It exposes what we have hidden, unearths what we have neglected, misremembered, denied. It is a method of capturing, of pinning down, but it is also a form of truth, of liberation.

If one is to unpack all the boxes, this is a novel, I believe, about language, about storytelling and its discontents. The disquieting message of *Ties* is not so much that life is fleeting, that we are alone in this world, that we hurt one another, that we grow old and forget, but that none of this can be captured, not even by means of literature. Containers may be the destiny of many in that they hold our remains after death. But this novel reminds us that narrative refuses to stay put, and that the effort of telling stories only pins things down so far. In the end it is language itself that is the most problematic container; it holds too much and too little at the same time.

I am deeply grateful to Domenico Starnone not only for the work he has produced but for inviting me and trusting me to translate it. It is with *Lacci* that I return to English after a hiatus of not working with the language for nearly four years. It is this project that has inspired me to reopen my English dictionaries, my old thesaurus, after a considerable period of neglect. My fear, before I began, was that it would distance me from Italian, but the effect has been quite the contrary. If anything I feel more tied to it than ever. I have encountered countless new words, new idioms, new ways of phrasing things. And though I translated the book in America it has also brought me closer in some sense to Rome, the city in which I was living when I discovered the book, the city in which much of the novel's action is set. It is in Rome, the city to which I will forever happily return, that I revised and completed the translation, and where I write these words of introduction.

These scattered observations cannot possibly contain my admiration for what Domenico Starnone has achieved in these pages. I am tempted to better organize my thoughts, but all I really want to say is: open this book. Read it, reread it. Discover the words, the voice, the sleight of hand of this brilliant writer.

BOOK ONE

CHAPTER ONE

1.

In case it's slipped your mind, Dear Sir, let me remind you: I am your wife. I know that this once pleased you and that now, suddenly, it chafes. I know you pretend that I don't exist, and that I never existed, because you don't want to look bad in front of the highbrow people you frequent. I know that leading an orderly life, having to come home in time for dinner, sleeping with me instead of with whomever you want, makes you feel like an idiot. I know you're ashamed to say: look, I was married on October 11th, 1962, at twenty-two; I said "I do" in front of the priest in a church in the Stella neighborhood, and I did it for love, nothing forced me into it; look, I have certain responsibilities, and if you people don't know what it means to have responsibilities you're petty. I know, believe me, I know. But whether you like it or not, the fact remains: I am your wife and you are my husband. We've been married for twelve years—twelve years in October—and we have two children: Sandro, born in 1965, and Anna, born in 1969. Do I need to show you their birth certificates to shake some sense into you?

Enough, sorry, I'm going overboard. I know you, I know you're a decent person. But please, as soon as you read this letter, come home. Or, if you still aren't up to it, write to me and explain what you're going through. I'll try to understand, I promise. It's already clear to me that you need more freedom, as it should be, so the children and I will try to burden you as little as possible. But you need to tell me word for word what's going on between you and this girl. It's been six days and you haven't called, you don't write, you don't turn up. Sandro asks me about you, Anna doesn't want to wash her hair because she says you're the only one who can dry it properly. It's not enough to swear that this woman, or girl, doesn't interest you, that you won't see her again, that she doesn't matter, that it was just the result of a crisis that's been building inside you for a while. Tell me how old she is, what her name is, if she works, if she studies, if she does nothing. I bet she was the one who kissed you first. I know you're incapable of making the first move, either they reel you in or you don't budge. And now you're stunned, I saw the look on your face when you told me: "I've been with another woman." Do you want to know what I think? I think you have yet to realize what you've done to me. It's as if you've stuck your hand down my throat and pulled, pulled, pulled to the point of ripping my heart out, don't you get it?

2.

Reading over what you write, I come off as the torturer and you the victim. I won't stand for this. I'm trying my best, I'm going to lengths you can't possibly imagine, and meanwhile you're the victim? Why? Because I raised my voice a bit, because I shattered the water carafe? You have to admit, I had my reasons. You turned up without warning after almost a month's absence. You seemed calm, even affectionate. I thought, thank god, he's back to himself again. Instead you told me, as if it were nothing, that the same person who, four weeks ago, didn't matter—to your credit, deciding it was time to give her a name, you called her Lidia—is now so important that you can't bear to live without her. Setting aside the moment in which you acknowledged her existence, you spoke to me as if it were a public service announcement and that all

I'd have to say was: okay, thanks, go off with this Lidia, I'll do my best to not bother you anymore. And as soon as I tried to react you stopped me, you went on to talk in abstract terms about the family: the family in history, the family in the world, your family of origin, ours. Was I supposed to shut up and be nice? Was that what you expected? You're ridiculous at times. You think it's enough to toss together general topics and some anecdote of yours to square things away. But I'm sick of your little games. You told me for the umpteenth time, in a pathetic tone you seldom use, how your parents' miserable marriage ruined your childhood. You used a dramatic image: you said that your father had wrapped barbed wire around your mother, and that every time you saw a sharp clump of iron pierce her flesh you suffered.

Then you moved on to us. You explained that just as your father had damaged all of you, so you—since the ghost of that unhappy man who made you all unhappy still torments you—were afraid of damaging Sandro, Anna and, most of all, me. See how I didn't miss a word of it? For a long time you reasoned with pedantic calm about the roles we were imprisoned in by getting married—husband, wife, mother, father, children—and you described us—me, you, our children—as gears in a senseless machine, bound always to repeat the same foolish moves. And so you carried on citing a book now and then to shut me up. At first I thought you were talking like that because something so terrible had happened to you that you no longer remembered who I was: a person with thoughts, feelings, a voice of her own, and not a puppet in your Pulcinello show. It dawned on me somewhat late that you were trying to be helpful. You wanted to make me realize that, by destroying the life we shared, you were in fact freeing me and the children, and that we should be grateful for your generosity. Oh, thank you, how kind of you. And you were offended because I threw you out of the house?

Aldo, please, think it over. We need to face one another, seriously; I need to understand what's happening to you. In our many years of living together you were always an affectionate man, both with me and the children. You're nothing like your father, I assure you, and all that stuff you said about the barbed wire, about the gears and other nonsense never occurred to me. Instead it's occurred to me—and this is true—that in recent years something about us has been changing, that you've been looking with interest at other women. I vividly remember the one at the campground, two summers ago. You were lying in the shade, reading for hours. You were busy, you said, and so you weren't paying attention to me or the children, you were studying under the pine trees or stretched out on the sand, writing. But when you looked up it was to look at her. And your mouth hung open a little, the way it does when you have a confusing thought in your head that you're trying to figure out.

At the time I told myself that you were doing nothing wrong: the girl was lovely, we can't control our eyes, sooner or later a glance slips out. But I suffered, acutely, especially when you started offering to do the dishes, something that never happened. You darted off toward the sinks as soon as she set out and returned when she came back. Do you think I'm blind, insensitive, that I didn't notice? I told myself: calm down, it doesn't mean anything. It seemed inconceivable to me that another woman might appeal to you, because I was convinced that if you were attracted to me once you'd be attracted to me forever. I believed real feelings never changed, especially in marriage. It happens, I told myself, but only to superficial people, and he isn't one. Then I told myself that it was an era of change; even you theorized that we needed to shake things up, that maybe I was too caught up in household chores, in managing our money, in the children's needs.

I started looking at myself secretly in the mirror. How was I, what was I? Two pregnancies had barely altered me, I was an efficient wife and mother. But evidently being almost identical to the time we'd met and fallen in love wasn't enough, to the contrary—maybe that was the mistake; what I had to do was reinvent myself, be more than just a good wife and mother. So I tried to look like the one at the camp, and like the girls that no doubt hovered around you in Rome, and I made an effort to participate more in your life outside the house. And a different phase began, slowly. I hope you noticed. Or no? You noticed but it didn't help? Why not? Didn't I do enough? Was I stuck midstream, unable to match up to the other women, always being who I was? Or did I go overboard? Did I change too much, did my transformation upset you? Were you ashamed of me, did you not recognize me anymore?

Let's talk about it, you can't leave me in the lurch. I need to know about this Lidia. Does she have her own place, do you sleep there? Does she have what you were looking for, what I no longer have, or never did? You snuck off, avoiding speaking to me clearly at all costs. Where are you? The address you left is in Rome, so is the phone number, but you don't respond when I write, the phone keeps ringing. What do I have to do to find you? Call one of your friends, come to the university? Start screaming in front of your colleagues and students? Do I have to let everyone know how irresponsible you are?

I have to pay the gas and the electricity. There's the rent. And two kids. Come back right away. They have the right to parents who take care of them day and night, a father and mother to have breakfast with in the mornings, who take them to school and pick them up again at the gates. They have the right to have a family, a family with a house where you eat lunch together and play and do homework and watch a little television and then have dinner and then watch some more television and then say goodnight. Say goodnight to Dad, Sandro, and you too, Anna, say goodnight to your father without whining, please. No fairy tale tonight, it's late; if you want a fairy tale then hurry up and brush your teeth, Dad will tell you one, but not more than fifteen minutes, then to bed, otherwise tomorrow you'll be late for school, besides your father has an early train to catch, if he shows up late they'll scold him. And the kids—do you no longer remember?—they run to brush their teeth, then come to you for the fairy tale, every night, the way it's been since they were born, the way it should be until they grow up, until they go off, and we grow old. But maybe you're no longer interested in growing old with me or even in watching your children grow up. Is that it? Is it?

I'm afraid. The house is isolated, you know how it is in Naples, it's a scary place. At night I hear noises, laughter, I don't sleep, I'm worn out. What if a thief gets in through the window? What if they steal the television, the record player? What if someone who's angry with you kills us in our sleep for revenge? Is it possible that you don't realize the weight you've dumped on top of me? Have you forgotten that I don't have a job, that I don't know how to get by? Don't make me lose my patience, Aldo, be careful. If I start to lose it, I'll make you pay.

3.

I saw Lidia. She's very young, beautiful, well-bred. She listened carefully to what I had to say about you. And she said something quite reasonable: you need to talk to him, I have nothing to do with your relationship. Indeed, she's a stranger, it was wrong of me to look for her. What could she have told me? That you fell for her, that you're taken by her, that you liked her, that you still like her? No, you're the only one who can explain every angle of this to me. She's nineteen. What does she know, understand? You're thirty-four, a married man, well-educated, you have a respectable job, you're highly regarded. It's up to you to give me a solid explanation, not Lidia. And yet all that you've told me, in two months, is that you can't live with us anymore. Right? And what's the reason? With me—you've sworn—there wasn't a problem. As for the children there was no arguing, they're your children. They get along well with you and you, by your own admission, with them. Well then? No reply. All you do is babble: I don't know, it happened. And when I ask if you have a new place, new books, your own things, you say no, I don't have anything, I'm a mess. And when I tell you, you live with Lidia, you sleep together, you eat together, you shrug it off, you mumble, no, of course not, we're seeing each other, that's all. I'd like to warn you, Aldo. Don't keep doing this, I can't take it. Each of our conversations rings false to me. Actually, I'd say that I'm making a concerted effort that's destroying me while you keep lying, and by lying you make clear that you no longer have any respect for me, that you're rejecting me.

I'm getting more scared. I'm scared that you'll contrive to transmit the spite you harbor toward me to the children, to our friends, to everyone. You want to isolate me, cut me out completely. And, what matters most, you want to avoid every attempt to reexamine our relationship. This is driving me crazy. I, unlike you, need to know; it's crucial that you tell me, point by point, why you've left. If you still consider me a human being and not an animal to ward off with a stick, you owe me an explanation, and it had better be a decent one.

4.

I get it now. You decided to pull out, abandoning us to our fate. You want your own life, there's no room for us. You want to go wherever you like, see whomever you wish, become the person you'd like to be. You long to leave our little world behind and join the great wide one with a new woman. In your view, we're proof of how you wasted your youth. You think of us as an illness that's kept you from growing, and without us you hope to make up for it.

If I've understood properly, you disapprove of my saying *us* so often. But that's how it is: the kids and I are *us,* and you, by now, are *you.* By walking away you've destroyed our life with you. You've destroyed how we once saw you, what we believed you were. You did so knowingly, planning it out, forcing us to realize that you were just a figment of our imagination. And now here were are: Sandro, Anna and I, subject to poverty, to an absolute lack of security, to despair, while you enjoy yourself, god knows where, with your lover. My children, as a result, are now mine alone; they don't belong to you. You've seen to it that their father has become an illusion to them, and to me.

Nevertheless you say you want to maintain a relationship. Fine, I don't object, the key is that you explain how. You want to be a father in every respect, even though you've shut me out of your life? You want to take care of Sandro and Anna, devote yourself to them without me? You want to be a shadow that materializes once in a while, and then you want to leave them to me? Ask the kids, see if it's OK with them. All I can say is that you've suddenly snatched away what they thought was theirs, and that this causes them a great deal of pain. Sandro thought of you as the center of his world and now he's flailing. Anna doesn't know what she's done wrong but she thinks that whatever it is it must be so serious that you've punished her by leaving. Welcome to the situation. I'll keep watch. But I'm telling you straight off that, first, I will not let you ruin my relationship with them and, second, I will prevent you from hurting my children any more than you already have by proving yourself to be a father who is utterly false.

5.

I hope it's clear to you now why the end of our relationship also entails the end of your relationship with Sandro and Anna. It's easy to say: I'm the father and I want to keep being one. In practice you've demonstrated that there's no room for the children in your current life, that you want to free yourself of them as you freed yourself of me. When, exactly, were you truly concerned for them?

Here's the latest, assuming that it interests you. We've moved. I couldn't make the rent with the money I had. We went to live with Gianna, making do. The kids had to change schools and make new friends. Anna suffers because she can't see Marisa anymore, and you know how much that meant to her. It was clear to you from the start that things would end up this way, that by leaving me you would subject them to all manner of discomfort and humiliation. But have you ever done a thing to avoid this? No, you've only thought of yourself.

You'd promised Sandro and Anna that you would spend the summer with them, the whole summer. You came half-heartedly one Sunday to get them, they were happy. But how did that end up? You brought them back to me after four days saying that looking after them put you on edge, that you didn't feel up to the task, and then you left with Lidia, not showing up again until the fall. You didn't bother yourself with what vacations they would have taken, where, how, with whom, with what money. Your needs were what counted, not those of your children.

But let's move on to the Sunday visits. You arrived late on purpose, you only stayed a few hours. You never took them out, you never played with them. You watched TV, and they were seated there beside you, expectant, watching you.

And the holidays? At Christmas, on New Year's, on the Epiphany, for Easter, you never got in touch. On the contrary, when the kids asked you explicitly to take them with you, you kept saying that you didn't have a place to put them, as if they were strangers. Anna drew you a picture of one of her ominous dreams and described it to you in detail. But you didn't blink, you weren't moved, you just sat there telling her, what pretty colors. You only perked up when, in the course of our discussions, you felt the need to highlight that you had your own life: that your life wasn't our life, and that the separation was final.

I know now that you're afraid. You fear that the children weaken your resolve to cut us out, that they get in the way of your new relationship, that they ruin it. Therefore, my dear, when you say you still want to be a father, it's just talk. The reality is something else: in freeing yourself of me, you also want to free yourself from your children. It's obvious that your critique of the family, of traditional roles and other drivel, is just an excuse. You're hardly fighting against an oppressive institution that reduces people to their assigned roles. If this were the case you'd realize that I agree with you, that I, too, want to free myself and change. If this were the case, once you'd dismantled the family, you'd pause at the edge of the emotional, economic and social cliff you're tossing us over and you would hasten to recognize our feelings, our desires. But no. You want to rid yourself of Sandro, Anna and me as people. You see us as an obstacle to your happiness, a trap that smothers your desire for pleasure. You consider us an irrational, malign residue. You've said it to yourself from the very beginning: I need to get a grip on myself, even if it kills them.

6.

You raise the example of the staircase. You say, you know when we go up the stairs? One foot after the other the way we learned when we were kids. But the joy of taking those first steps has disappeared. Growing up, we were molded by the strides of our parents, our older siblings, the people we're tied to. Now our legs move according to acquired habits. And the tension, the emotion, the happiness of each step must have perished along with the uniqueness of our stride. We proceed believing that the movement of our legs is our own, but it isn't so; there's a small crowd that's shaped us, moving up those steps with us, and the steadiness of our legs simply stems from conformity. Either we change our step—you conclude—rediscovering the joys of starting out, or we condemn ourselves to the dread of normality.

Have I summarized it well? Now can I give you my opinion? It's a stupid metaphor, you can do better. Nevertheless, I'll indulge you. In your usual overwrought way you wanted me to know that we were once happy, but that our happiness gave way to routines that, on the one hand, enabled days, months and years to pass by without much trouble but, on the other hand, suffocated both of us, as well as the children. Great. But now you have to tell me what the upshot is. Do you mean that, were it possible, you'd gladly go back fifteen years, but that one can't go back, and furthermore your thirst for a new beginning is so powerful that your only resort is to restart with Lidia? Is this what you mean? If so, I want to tell you something. I too, for some time, have felt that the joys of the past have faded. I too, for some time, have thought we've changed, and that this change hurts you, me, Sandro, and Anna, that the whole family runs the risk of leading a tortured life under one roof. I too, for some time, have feared that if we're reduced to limping along together and raising our children, we act against ourselves and against them, and that therefore it's best that I leave you. But I, *I*, unlike you, don't believe it's your fault we lost the keys to earthly paradise, and that therefore I'd better hook up with someone less absent-minded. I don't obliterate the three of you, I don't deny your existence, even to free myself. And to free myself how, exactly? By forming another couple and another family the way you're doing with Lidia?

Aldo, please, don't play with words, I'm worn out, it's the last time I'm going to try to talk sense into you. Regretting the past is stupid, just as it's stupid to keep running after new beginnings. Your desire for change has one possible outlet, the four of us: me, you, Sandro, Anna. It's our duty to take a new step, together. Look at me, really look at me, please look at me when you see me. I'm not nostalgic about anything. I'm trying to climb up your wretched steps in my own way, and I want to move forward. But if you don't give me or the children a chance, I'm going to court, and I'll ask for full custody.

7.

You've finally made an unequivocal move. You didn't flinch before the judge's order, you did nothing to reclaim the father-hood you kept invoking. You accepted that I alone would care for the children, disregarding the fact that they might need you. You've dumped their lives onto me, officially distancing them from your own. And because silence amounts to consent, these minors have been entrusted to me. *Effective immediately.* Bravo, you make me so proud of having loved you.

8.

I killed myself. I know I should write, *I tried to kill myself*, but that would be inaccurate. For all intents and purposes, I died. Do you think I did it to force you to come back? Is that why, even under those circumstances, you were careful not to show up for even five minutes in the hospital? Were you afraid

of getting backed into a corner? Or were you afraid of looking
straight-on at the mess you'd made?

Jesus, you really are a weak and confused man: insensitive,
superficial, the opposite of what I thought you were for twelve
years. You're not interested in people, in how they change,
how they evolve. You use people. You only accommodate them
if they put you on a pedestal. You're only fond of them as long
as they grant you prestige and a role that's worthy of you, only
as long as, by celebrating you, they prevent you from seeing
that you're actually empty, and afraid of your emptiness. Every
time this mechanism jams, every time people step back and try
to grow, you destroy them and move on. You're never still, you
always need to be at the center of something. You say it's
because you want to be a man of your times. You call this
frenzy of yours involvement. Oh, sure, you're involved, you
take part, you take part a little too much. But really you're a
passive man, you pick up words and ideas from books that
appeal to the masses and you put them in play, you're entirely
subject to the conventions and trends of people who matter,
whom you quickly hope to associate with. You're never yourself, when have you ever been? You don't even know what it
means. You're only trained to take advantage of opportunities
when and if they arise. In Rome you were offered a lectureship
at the university and so you started to be a lecturer. Student
protests hit, and so you started getting political. Your mother
died, she was clingy, and since I was there in the role of your
girlfriend, you married me. You had kids but only because,
once you were a husband, you thought you needed to be a
father too, because that's what one does. You came across a
respectable young girl close at hand and in the name of sexual
liberation and the dissolution of the family you became her
lover. You'll go on like this forever, you'll never be what you
want, just what happens by chance.

I've tried, throughout this whole hellish period—three

years of torment—to be helpful to you. I struggled night and day to examine myself, and I urged you to do the same. You didn't notice. You listened to me, distracted; I'm almost certain you've never even read my letters. While I recognized that, yes, the family is suffocating, that the roles it imposes obliterate us—while as a result I was making a herculean effort to arrive at the crux of the matter, changing, changing and evolving in every way—you didn't even realize it. And if you did realize, you were disgusted, you scurried away, you destroyed me with barely a word, a look, a gesture. The suicide, my dear, was validation. You killed me a while back, not in my role as wife but as a human being who was in her richest, most sincere moment. That I in fact survived, that according to public records I'm still living, isn't fortunate for me—not at all—but for my children. Your absence, your lack of interest even at this critical juncture have proven to me that, had I died, you would have gone your own way in any case.

9.

I'm answering the questions you ask.

In the past two years I've worked in various capacities, for generally little pay, both in the public and private sector. It's only of late that I have a steady job.

Our separation is, by definition, sanctioned by official family records and by the declaration of custody that you signed. I don't see the need for further steps.

I regularly receive the money you send, though I've never asked you for anything, not for myself, not for my children. I try, within the bounds of my financial circumstances, not to touch it, setting it aside for Sandro and Anna.

The television hasn't worked for ages and I've stopped paying fees.

You write that you need to reestablish a relationship with the children. You believe, now that four years have gone by, that it's possible to face the problem calmly. But what is there left to face? Wasn't the nature of your need precisely defined when you absented yourself, robbing us of our life? When you abandoned them because you couldn't handle the responsibility? In any case I've read them your request and they've decided to meet you. I remind you, in case you've forgotten, that Sandro is thirteen, and Anna nine. They're crushed by uncertainty and fear. Don't make it worse for them.

BOOK TWO

CHAPTER ONE

1.

Let's proceed in order. Shortly before we left for vacation, Vanda, who had a wrist fracture that wasn't healing, consulted her orthopedist and rented an electronic stimulator for two weeks. She'd settled with the company on a price of two hundred and five euros, and it was supposed to be delivered within twenty-four hours. And so the following day around noon the doorbell rang, and since my wife was busy in the kitchen, I went to open the door, led, as usual, by the cat. A young woman, thin, her short black hair perhaps a bit lank. Lively eyes—without makeup—dominated a pale, delicate face. She handed over a gray box. I took the package, telling her that my wallet was on the desk in my study. Just a moment, please, I said. She followed me into the house, though I hadn't invited her to enter.

—Gorgeous, she said, addressing the cat. What's his name?

—Labes, I replied.

—What kind of name is that?

—It's short for *la bestia*, the beast.

The girl laughed and, kneeling down, stroked Labes.

—It's two hundred and ten euros, she said.

—Wasn't it two hundred and five?

She shook her head, still totally charmed by the cat, tickling him under the throat and murmuring sweet nothings. Then, still crouched down, she spoke to me with the gentle tone of someone who, going from house to house for work, knows how to placate the anxieties of old people when a stranger knocks at the door. Open the box, she said, the bill's inside, you'll see that it's two-ten. And all the while, tickling the cat, her eyes were roaming, curious, past the door of my study.

—Lots of books.

—They're for my work.

—Must be a nice job. And so many figurines. That cube up there is an amazing blue, is it wooden?

—Metal. I bought it in Prague, years ago.

—You have a lovely place, she said, straightening. Then she motioned once more to the box. Have a look.

I liked the light in her eyes.

—It's fine, I said, and gave her two hundred and ten euros. She took the money and said bye to the cat, warning me:

—Don't knock yourself out reading. See you later, Labes.

—Goodbye, thank you, I said.

That was it, nothing more, nothing less. After a few minutes Vanda came out of the kitchen wearing a green apron that nearly reached her feet. She opened the box, stuck the plug into the charger, checked that the generator was working, and examined the solenoid to figure out how to use it. I, in the meantime, out of curiosity, glanced at the bill. The girl had cheated me.

—Something wrong? asked my wife, who notices when my mood changes even when she's distracted.

—They wanted two hundred and ten euros.

—And you gave it to them?

—Yes.

—I'd told you, two hundred and five.

—Seemed like an honest person.

—Was it a woman?

—A girl.

—Pretty?

—I guess.

—A miracle she only filched five.

—Five euros isn't a huge amount.

—Five euros were ten thousand lire in the old days. Tightening her lips, which is what she does when she's irritated, she went on to study the instructions. She's hung up on money. She's been obsessed with saving it all her life. Even today, in spite of all her aches and pains, she's quick to bend over and pick up one cent from the grubby sidewalk. She's one of those people who never neglects to emphasize, as a reminder intended above all to themselves, that a euro is worth two thousand lire and that if, fifteen years ago, two people spent twelve thousand lire to go to the movies, today, at eight euros a ticket, they spend thirty-two thousand. Our current wellbeing, and to some extent that of our children, who frequently ask us for money, is owed less to my job than to her toughness. As a result, the fact that a stranger, a few minutes ago, appropriated five of our euros must have galled her as much as it would have thrilled her to find the same amount next to a parked car.

As is often the case, her disappointment aggravated my own. I'm going to write an email to the company, I said, and I withdrew into my study with the intention of reporting this little scam. I wanted to calm my wife down; her disapproval has always plagued me, never mind the sarcasm about how, at my age, I'm still foolishly prey to sweet-talk from women. And so, turning on the computer, I mulled over the gestures, voice and words of the delivery girl. I thought again about the appealing way she'd said, gorgeous cat, lots of books, and I remembered the solicitous, almost tender way she'd urged me to open the package and check inside. Apparently one look was enough to tell her that it would be easy to cheat me.

Realizing it bothered me. I mentally traced a line between how I would have reacted a few years ago (*don't waste my time, this is the amount we'd agreed upon, goodbye*) and how I'd reacted now (*the cat's named Labes, the books are for my work,*

I bought the cube in Prague, it's fine, thanks). So I resolved to type up a few harsh sentences. But a perplexing lack of motivation soon settled over me. I thought: who knows how this girl gets by: precarious, poorly paid jobs, parents to support, an exorbitant rent, the need to buy makeup and a pair of tights, an unemployed husband or boyfriend, problems with drugs. If I write to the company, I told myself, no doubt she'll lose this little gig, too. What were five euros in the end? A tip that, behind my wife's back, I'd have gladly given her. And besides, if, in these economically depressed times, the girl keeps going around inflating prices for her own gain, soon enough she'll find someone who's less forgiving than I am, who'll make her pay for it.

I gave up on the letter. I told Vanda that I'd sent it and then I forgot about the whole episode.

2.

A few days later we left for the sea. My wife packed the bags and I dragged them downstairs, to the car. It was scorching hot. The street, usually busy with cars, was empty. The surrounding buildings were silent, the windows and balconies shielded, for the most part, by bars and lowered shutters.

I was covered in sweat from the effort. Vanda wanted to help and since I told her not to—I was worried that her bones were too fragile—she gave me instructions about how to arrange the suitcases. She was nervous; leaving the apartment made her anxious. Though we were just spending seven days by the sea in a hotel near Gallipoli—bed and breakfast at a decent price, nothing to do other than sleep, walk along the shore, enjoy a swim—she kept saying that she would have gladly stayed at home to read on the balcony between the lemon tree and the medlar.

We've lived in this house for three decades and every time
we have to leave it she acts as if she'll never come back to it
again. Over the years convincing her to treat us to a little
break has become increasingly complicated. In the first
place, she believes she's wronging the children, the grandchildren. But above all she doesn't like to leave Labes; she
loves him and he loves her. I, too, needless to say, am fond of
our pet, but not to the point of letting it ruin my vacation.
And so I have to convince her, cautiously, that the cat will
damage the furniture in the hotel, trample through our room,
bother the other guests with his nocturnal mewing. And
when she finally resigns herself to the separation I have to
make sure that the kids will drop by to fill the bowl and clean
out the litter box. This tends to distress her considerably.
The kids don't get along well, and it's usually best to avoid
forcing brother and sister to meet, for whatever reason.
There were always tensions between them, from early adolescence on, but things got worse about a dozen years ago,
when their aunt Gianna died. Vanda's older sister, in the
course of her troubled life, didn't have children, and she was
particularly fond of Sandro, so in the end she left him a handsome nest egg and Anna some knickknacks of negligible
value. A dispute was born. Anna demanded that the last
wishes of her aunt be ignored and that the inheritance be
divided equally; Sandro refused. As a result they don't see
each other anymore, something that, along with the myriad
other problems in their haphazard lives, makes their mother
suffer deeply. In order to avoid that they even cross paths
when they're taking care of Labes, therefore, I study the
turns and schedules, and Vanda, who has no faith in my orga-
nizational skills, oversees them, making sure that each child
has the keys to our apartment. This is just to explain how
laborious it all is. But now here we are, she and I, with our
luggage. We've lived together for fifty-two years, a vast

length of coiled time. Vanda, seventy-six, is an artificially
energetic lady, and I, at seventy-four, am an artificially distracted man. She has always organized my life without dis-
sembling, and I have always followed her orders without
protesting. She's quite active in spite of her aches and pains,
and I'm lazy in spite of my good health. I've already put the
red suitcase in the trunk, but my wife objects, she doesn't
agree, better to put the black one below and the red one on
top. I unstuck the shirt from my back with my finger, I pulled
out the red suitcase. I put it down on the asphalt, with an
exaggerated groan, in order to pick up the black one. It was
then that a car pulled up.

It was impossible not to notice, given that not only the
street but the entire city seemed empty, the traffic lights uselessly changing colors. You could even hear the birds chirping
in the treetops. The car pulled up beside us, a few feet away,
blocking us in. A second, two: I distinctly heard the sound of
the gears shifting. After the rapid whine of reverse, it stopped
where we were.

—No way, exclaimed the man seated at the wheel, his eyes
recessed, his teeth starting to age. I'm driving along and what
do you know: you, it's really you, here on the street, just like
that. When I tell my dad he'll never believe it.

He was animated, chuckling with contentment. I put down
the black suitcase and tried to conjure up some trait of his—
the nose, the mouth, the forehead—that would help me to
remember who he was. But I couldn't, the emotions playing
across his face caused his features to blur. And he spoke without stopping, he showered me with a torrent of words about
his father, who remembered me with respect and affection, and
about certain difficulties I'd helped him deal with when he was
a boy, and about how finally things were okay, in fact they
seemed to be getting better. He kept saying, It's so great to see
you. And though I had no idea if it was him I'd helped out, or

the father, or both, I quickly convinced myself that he must have been one of my students, maybe during that brief phase of my youth when I'd taught at a high school in Naples, or maybe the longer phase when I'd taught at the university in Rome. It often happen that I encountered cheerful, unknown people, and in their adult faces, often quite marked, I sometimes recognized—though, more often than not, I only pretended to recognize—former students. Yes, I concluded, it's the most likely story, he must be a former student. I didn't want to hurt this man by not recognizing him. I put on a cordial look, I concluded by asking:

—And how is your father?

—Fine. He has some trouble with his heart, it's nothing serious.

—Tell him hello.

—Of course.

—And you, things are going well?

—I'm great. You remember, right, that I wanted to go to Germany? Well I went and I'm finally having some luck. What are the options in Italy? Nil. In Germany, on the other hand, I set up a little factory. I work with leather, I make bags, jackets—quality merchandise that sells.

—I'm happy for you. You're married?

—Not yet, I'm getting married in the fall.

—I wish you all the best, and again, say hello to your father.

—Thanks, you have no idea how happy he'll be.

I waited for him to leave but he didn't. We stayed like that for a few seconds, with smiles glued to our faces, without saying a word. Then he started shaking his head:

—No, wait, who knows when we'll see each other again. I'd at least like to give you and your wife a gift.

—Another time, we have to go now.

—It'll just take a second, I'll get it right away.

The man got out of his car. He was speedy, decisive. He

opened his trunk. Here, he said to Vanda, handing her a shiny little purse that she accepted uneasily, as if it would soil her. Meanwhile, the stranger had selected a black leather jacket, and he held it up against me, saying, it's perfect. I tried to fend him off, saying, it's too much, I can't accept. But he went on, turning back to Vanda, wanting to give her a jacket as well, with shiny clasps. It's just your size, he said, satisfied with himself. At that point I tried to stop him. You've been very kind, thanks again, but enough with the gifts, it's getting late, we'll hit traffic. At this he changed; the face, slippery until now, stiffened.

—Please, it's nothing, a guy does what he can. I'm only asking a small favor, a few euros for gas, I need to get to Germany, it's not necessary though, if you think it's too much don't worry, the gifts remain gifts.

I was bewildered: the father, the gratitude, the little German factory, the business going smoothly, and now he wanted a few euros for gas? I reached mechanically for my wallet, looking for five euros, ten, but all I had was a hundred-euro note. Sorry, I muttered, but meanwhile my forehead was pounding. I was about to say to him: As a matter of fact I'm not at all sorry, take back your stuff and get out of here. It took an instant. With a precise gesture, like quicksilver, the man descended on my wallet, squeezing together his thumb and index finger, his digits clasping the hundred euros, snatching them from me with a polite look of gratitude. The next minute he was behind the wheel, calling out, Thank you, Dad will be so pleased.

If the scam involving the girl with the solenoid had only embittered me, this episode pained me. The car still hadn't faded from view at the end of the street when my wife, incredulous, exclaimed:

—You gave him a hundred euros?

—I didn't give him anything, he took it.

—This stuff isn't worth a penny. Smell it, it stinks. It's not leather, it stinks of cod.

—Throw it all out in the dumpster.

—No, I'll give them to the Red Cross.

—Fine.

—No, it's not fine. We were raised in Naples for God's sake, and you let yourself get scammed like this?

3.

I drove for hours, to the sea, nauseated by the stench of the jacket and the purse. Vanda couldn't get over it. A hundred euros, she kept saying, two hundred thousand lire, how can it have happened? But then her irritation died down, she drew a deep breath of resignation and said, fine, oh well, let's not think about it anymore. I nodded at once and tried to say something just as decisive. But I didn't come up with anything convincing and meanwhile I started to feel as if any blow might shatter me. The fault, I think, of the connection I'd established almost instantly between the dark-haired delivery girl and the swindler with aging teeth. For both of them—I thought—one look was enough for them to say: Here we go, this one's easy. And they'd been right, I'd fallen for it. Evidently my alarm system was worn out to the point of being deactivated. Or, who knows, over the years the mark of a man you don't fool with— a certain look, a scowl—had faded. Or, put more simply, it was as if I'd gone foggy, having lost the vigilant elasticity that, in the course of my life, had enabled me to escape my meager origins, to raise children, to thrive in difficult situations, to earn myself a little prosperity, to adjust for good or for ill to the circumstances. I didn't know precisely how or to what degree I'd changed, but it now seemed clear that I had.

We'd almost reached our destination when I received

another slight confirmation that I was in danger of losing control of the entire delicate system of weights and counterweights that had kept my life in check for five decades. While I reluctantly navigated the heedless summer traffic, I tried to remember whether I'd ever been cheated in the past, but nothing came to mind. Instead a detail resurfaced from long ago when I'd been the one to come out on top. Breaking a long silence and, without preamble, in keeping with my thoughts, I recounted to Vanda, who was half-asleep with her forehead against the glass, the time—it had surely been spring—that she'd gone with me to the RAI studios. I don't remember now exactly what year it had been, or why: Maybe, I said, it wasn't even RAI, maybe I wasn't working there anymore, who knows where we'd gone. But what was certain was that at the end of the taxi ride I'd paid the driver with a fifty-thousand lire note, that he'd claimed it was ten thousand, and that we'd started to bicker. The man was even rude to my wife, who had clearly seen the fifty thousand and wanted to back me up. I became haughty as I knew how to be. I asked the driver his first name, last name, and so on, and then I declared that he could keep the fifty thousand but that I was about to go to the carabinieri. First he spat out all the details, gruffly, and then he started muttering: I shouldn't have gone out today, why the hell did I? I have the flu. In the end he gave me the right change. Remember that? I asked her, proud of myself.

My wife roused herself. She looked at me, perplexed.

—You're mixing things up, she said, coldly.

—That's just how it happened.

—I wasn't in the taxi with you.

I instantly felt a flush shooting up my chest, burning my forehead. I chased it back down.

—Of course you were there.

—Enough.

—You're the one who doesn't remember.

—I said enough.

—Maybe I was alone, I muttered, and then, abruptly, I stopped talking, just as abruptly as I'd started.

What little was left of the journey passed in sulky silence. Our spirits lifted only when we arrived at the hotel, when we were given a room that overlooked the beach, and the ocean. Dinner that night was excellent, and once we came back to the room we discovered that the air conditioner was blissfully quiet, and that the mattress and pillows were ideal for cushioning Vanda's bad back. We took our medications and sank into a deep sleep.

Little by little I cheered up. The weather was lovely all seven days, the water transparent. We went for long swims, took long walks. The countryside and the houses were airy. The sea, at certain times of day, revealed a greenish-blue that sparkled under the strong sun. The sunsets were scarlet. Even though, at the buffet, both at lunch and dinner, there was savage competition among the guests to see who piled on the most food, and Vanda reproached me for barely filling my plate, and the room reverberated unpleasantly with the cries of adults and children, and after eleven at night the waiters startled us, warning us not to go to the beach because it was dangerous, to the point of barricading our sleep behind an impressive number of gates leading both to the sea and the street, all the same, we had a lovely vacation.

—What a nice breeze.

—I haven't seen water like this in years.

—Mind the jellyfish.

—Have you seen jellyfish?

—No, I don't think so.

—Then why scare me?

—I'm just saying.

—Or to ruin my swim.

—Don't be silly.

At Vanda's insistence we were even able to get an umbrella in the first row. In the shade, stretched out in chairs facing the drowsy sea, my wife read books on scientific predictions, telling me, now and then, about the subatomic world or outer space, while I read novels and poems that I shared with her softly from time to time, not so much to read them to her but to grant myself further pleasure. After dinner, on the terrace, we both often happened to see the wake of a falling star at the same moment, and this delighted us. We admired the night sky, the fragrance of the air, and by midweek not only that beach, that sea, but the entire planet seemed a miracle. In the days that remained I felt quite wonderful. I savored the fortune of being, for a good seventy-four years, a happy transmutation of the sidereal substance that roils in the furnace of the universe, a fragment of living thinking matter, without too many aches and pains to boot, and barely scathed, purely by chance, by misfortune. The only bother was the mosquitoes that bit at night, me mostly, leaving Vanda in peace, so much so that she claimed there weren't any. Apart from that, how wonderful it was to live, to have lived. I marveled at my own optimism, a sentiment I have little calling for.

Alas, the very day we were leaving—at six in the morning to avoid the traffic—things took a turn. The sky grew cloudy and we traveled all the way back under fat, heavy drops of rain, and between the lightning and the impressive thunder the highways were far more dangerous than they'd been on the way there. I drove the whole time, as I had going (Vanda's a terrible driver), even though I repeatedly felt I no longer knew how to keep to the road, and, especially on the curves, feared I'd end up in the truck lane or against the guardrail.

—Shouldn't you slow down?

—I'm not speeding.

—Pull over and wait for it to stop raining.

—It won't stop.

—Good God, look at the lightning.

—Now you'll hear thunder.

—Do you think it's raining in Rome, too?

—I don't know.

—Labes is scared of thunder.

—He'll be OK.

My wife who, at the sea, had mentioned the cat only when she called Sandro and Anna to make sure everything was fine, now talked about him, worried, the whole way. Labes represented the tranquility of the house to which she, all the while torturing me for my reckless driving, couldn't wait to return. Her anxiety mounted when we discovered that, even in Rome, it was raining violently. The water flowed, filthy, at the sides of the roads, pooling in large dark wells in front of manholes. We parked on our street at two in the afternoon. It was oppressively hot in spite of the rain. I unloaded the bags. Vanda wanted to hold up the umbrella for me, but since we were both getting wet I told her to go in. After protesting a little she agreed, and I loaded myself down with the bags and the suitcases, arriving, soaked, at the elevator. My wife, who'd already gone up, yelled down from the landing:

—Leave the bags and come up right away.

—What happened?

—I can't open the door.

4.

I didn't pay her much attention. If Vanda has to wait a few minutes, I thought, the world won't come to end, and I reorganized the luggage in the elevator while replying calmly, —Coming, I'll be right there—to her increasingly pressing requests. It was only when I heaped the suitcases and bags on the landing that I realized how truly scared she was. She'd unlocked with the keys but there was something wrong. Look, she said, gesturing towards the door, half-open. I pushed, but nothing much happened; it was jammed. Then with a painful twist of the neck I stuck my head into the small space there was.

—Well? asked Vanda, distraught, holding me by the shirt as if she were afraid I'd fall in.

—It's a huge mess.

—Where?

—Inside.

—Who did it?

—I don't know.

—I'm calling Sandro.

I reminded her that our children were by now on vacation: Sandro had surely left that morning for France with Corinne's children, and who knew where Anna was. I'm calling anyway, said my wife, who trusts her son more than me, and started looking in her purse for her cell phone. But then suddenly she gave up. She remembered Labes, calling for him loudly, with authority. We waited: no noise, no mewing. Then, together, we pushed the door, and because we persisted, after a certain scraping sound against the floor, the sliver widened. I entered the house.

The foyer, usually tidy, was unrecognizable. The sofa and the living room table had ended up one on top of the other, as if dragged down by a tidal wave. Anna's old desk was leaning on one side. The drawers were pulled out—or had been pulled out—and were on the floor, one upright, the others overturned among old notebooks, pencils, pens, compasses, T squares and dolls that belonged, in childhood and in adolescence, to our daughter.

I took a few cautious steps, but I immediately felt a crunching underfoot, fragments of what remained of various knick-knacks. My wife called out, Aldo, Aldo, what's going on, are you okay? I examined the door. Some of the debris that was scattered on the floor was stuck under it. I pulled a piece free and opened the door wide. Vanda came into the house, unsteadily, as if fearing she'd trip and fall. She'd turned quite pale, her tan had become a greenish mask of clay. Since it looked like she was about to faint I gripped her by the arm. But she shook me off, saying nothing, heading quickly toward the living room, the rooms once occupied by our children, the kitchen, the bathroom, the bedroom.

I held back. In general, faced with difficult situations, I slow down; I try to avoid making the wrong moves. She, on the other hand, after a moment of bewilderment, dives headfirst into terror, fighting it with everything she's got. She's always behaved this way, ever since I've known her, and it was what she did now. While I listened to her footsteps in the hallway, crossing the rooms, I felt once more, with greater impact, that I was fragile and that I could crack. I looked around, I stuck my head into my study, mindful not to trample the prints that, until a week ago, had graced the walls, and that now lay on the floor among broken glass, shattered frames, toppled shelves, tattered books, fragments of vinyl records. I was still there, gathering up an old landscape of Capri, when Vanda came back. What are you doing? she asked, deranged. Don't just stand there, come look, it's a disaster. But meanwhile she previewed, in words, the scene of devastation: emptied-out closets, hangers and clothes strewn all over the place, our mattress upended, a furious rage turned upon all the mirrors in the house. The shutters were pulled up, the windows and balconies wide open. God knows how many creatures had come in, lizards, geckoes, maybe mice. She burst into tears.

I dragged her into the foyer again. I moved the desk into a corner, and unburdened the table that was leaning against the sofa, setting it back onto the floor. I put the sofa on its feet, I made her sit down. Stay here, I told her, unable to curb the irritation in my voice, and I went from one room to the next, increasingly dumbfounded. Every room had been turned upside down. It would take days, lots of work and money to make the apartment even remotely livable again. The CD player had ended up on the floor along with shiny discs, old documents once organized in folders and shells—so many shells that Anna used to collect when she was little, and that we'd stored in cardboard boxes—reduced to bits by the sole of a shoe. Everywhere, in the living room, in my study, in the kids' rooms, I found old furniture that we were fond of, trashed. And the bathroom? A pigsty: medicines, cotton pads, toilet paper, squeezed-out toothpaste, shards of the mirror, liquid soap everywhere. I felt the weight of the pain, but not mine; Vanda's. She was the one who cared for the house as if it were a living thing, who kept it clean and organized, who'd obliged me and the children, though the years, to respect draconian but nevertheless useful rules so that everything could always be found in its proper place. I went back to her. She was sitting in the gloom of the foyer.

—Who did it?

—Thieves, Vanda.

—To steal what? There's nothing of value.

—Exactly.

—What do you mean?

—They didn't find anything and they destroyed the house.

—How did they get in? The door was locked.

—Through the balconies, the windows.

—There were fifty euros in the kitchen drawer, did they take them?

—I don't know.

—And my mother's string of pearls?

—I don't know.

—Where is Labes?

5.

The cat, right. Where was he? Vanda leapt up, calling for him, nearly in a rage. I did, too, half-heartedly. We went from room to room, we went up to the windows, the balconies, shouting his name. Maybe he fell, my wife said quietly. We were on the third floor, and below us was the rough stone of the courtyard. No, I reassured her, he must be lost, he must be hiding. Afraid of the strangers who had entered the house. Afraid and repulsed, like us now, at the thought of unknown people touching our things. My wife suddenly wondered, what if they killed him? And she didn't wait for me to answer, I saw it in her eyes: Yes, they've killed him. She stopped calling him. She came back and looked frenetically through the house. She pushed things aside, she slipped in between overturned furniture, she examined what was still standing. I tried to get ahead of her. The thieves might have done to Labes the same thing they'd done, with unleashed fury, to our things. I preferred to find the body first and, if need be, hide it from her. I went to check the little room where we keep our winter clothes, and for a few seconds I was certain that I saw the animal hanged and quartered, as if in a horror movie, among the coats. Instead I found myself facing the usual debacle: the metal pole yanked out, clothing on the floor. No trace of Labes.

Vanda looked relieved. Not only could she return to thinking that the cat was still alive, but in the course of her exploration she'd discovered, to her surprise, in the very drawer in which she kept it, her mother's string of pearls—the only piece of jewelry she ever allowed herself—and under the sink, covered in a layer of detergent, the fifty euros she'd stashed in the kitchen cupboard. Suddenly the thieves seemed stupid to her. They'd rummaged everywhere, they'd shattered everything looking for god knows what treasures, but they hadn't found the little they might have stolen: the string of pearls, the fifty euros. Well, I comforted her, let's stop wearing ourselves out. I went back to look out over the balcony of my study, and the one that gave off the living room, to understand how they'd climbed up to the third floor, and meanwhile, without being obvious, I looked for traces of Labes in the courtyard. What was that dark stain on the roof of the first floor? Blood that endured in spite of the hot rain?

I convinced myself that the thieves—two or three?—had climbed the gutter up to the cornice and then, passing from there, reached our balcony. The shutter had been pulled up by hand, they'd taken the worn glass door off its hinges without breaking the glass and come in. We should have installed bars, I said to myself with regret, glancing around at the surrounding windows and balconies. But why protect yourself if you have nothing to protect? I came back in. In that moment the silence of the empty building was what afflicted me, more than the devastated house. Neither my wife nor I was able to vent, to show someone the damage and the insult we'd withstood, to receive some solidarity and advice, to feel bolstered by a little sympathy. Most of our neighbors were still on vacation. Not a footstep or a voice could be heard, doors didn't slam. The rainy grayness cancelled everything. Vanda must have read my thoughts. She said, Bring the bags in, I'm going to see if Nadar's here. And she didn't wait for me to say yes; it was clear that she could no longer stand being alone with me in the house. I heard her going down the stairs. She stopped on the first floor and knocked on our neighbor's door. He was a long-time friend, the only one in the building who almost never went on vacation.

I pulled our bags inside. In the chaos of the house they seemed to me the only clump of order, our only possessions—though the suitcases mostly contained dirty laundry—that weren't contaminated. I distinctly heard my wife's voice, and that of our neighbor. She was speaking in an agitated way,

Nadar interrupting her now and then with the shrill voice of a well-bred person. He was a retired judge, ninety-one, a very polite man, sharp as a tack in spite of his years. I returned to the landing and looked down the stairwell. Nadar was propped up by a cane. I saw the tufts of white hair on the sides of his skull. He was saying comforting things, using an elaborate syntax and the loud voice of deaf people. He was trying to be helpful. He'd heard some noises, not in the middle of the night, but rather, in the evening. He'd thought it was thunder, it had rained in Rome until yesterday nonstop. On the other hand, he was certain that he'd distinctly heard a mewing. It had gone on all night.

—Where? my wife asked, pressing him.

—In the courtyard.

Vanda raised her head, seeing me at the top of the steps.

Come down, she shouted, Nadar heard mewing in the courtyard.

I joined her reluctantly; had it been up to me I'd have closed up the house and gone back to the sea. Nadar wanted to come with us to look for Labes even though I insisted that he stay inside, as it was raining again. We wandered through the courtyard, all three of us calling for the cat. I wasn't able to focus. I thought: Thank God the water washed away every trace of the blood. I thought: We won't find him, he's hidden himself well in order to die in peace. Meanwhile I was looking at our neighbor, slight, bent, the pink skin of his face deeply creased on his forehead and cheekbones. Was that man my future, if indeed I had that much future left? Another twenty years. Twenty: me and Vanda, Vanda and me, sometimes Sandro with the children, sometimes Anna. We needed to put the house in order, get it back in shape, not waste time this way.

Nadar slapped his forehead. He'd thought of something important. He said to me:

—They were ringing your bell a lot, the past few days.

—Who?

—I don't know, But I heard the intercom.

—Of our apartment?

—Yes.

I said, jokingly:

—You hear the intercom of our apartment but not the thieves who demolish it?

—Deafness, he said by way of explanation. He was used to paying utmost attention to slight noises, and little or none to loud ones.

—How many times did they buzz?

—Five, six. One afternoon I came out.

—And who was it?

—A girl.

Since Nadar would also define my wife as a girl, I asked him to describe her to me. He was vague.

—Small, brown-haired, thirty years old at the most. She said she had to put flyers into the mailbox. I didn't open up for her.

—You're certain that she buzzed our place?

—Quite certain.

—And then?

—Then last night.

—It was her again?

—I don't know, there were two of them.

—Two girls?

—A man and a woman.

Vanda motioned to me. She was next to the fountain. Her green eyes were prominent on her gaunt face. She said:

—There's a dead bird here.

Only I understood what she meant. Labes is an impressive hunter of anything that flies. I left Nadar and joined her. Her white hair was stuck to her head because of the rain. It doesn't mean anything, I told her. Go back upstairs, meanwhile I'll go to the carabinieri. But she shook her head energetically, she wanted to come along. Our neighbor, who continued to assume the authority of a judge even though he'd been retired for twenty years, maintained that he might be of use there. He lined up behind us.

6.

We showed up under dripping umbrellas at the nearest carabinieri station and were welcomed into a tiny office by a well-mannered boy in uniform. Nadar introduced himself right away: first name, last name—Nadar Marossi—and above all his position: president of the court of appeals. He briefly recounted what had happened, and he did so with a commanding precision, but then tacked on a story about himself and his career in the course of various complex phases of the twentieth century. The young carabiniere listened as if he'd descended to hell to hear the idle chatter of the dead.

I tried various times to insert myself into Nadar's stories and to steer the conversation back toward the state in which we'd found the apartment, but when I finally managed I couldn't resist; the heroic role of our neighbor had annoyed me, and I wanted to convey to the boy that I, too, was someone special. So I repeated my name to the carabiniere two or three times—Aldo Minori, Aldo Minori, Aldo Minori—to see if it made an impression on him. Since the young man didn't react, I ended up talking about a TV series from the eighties that I'd created practically on my own, that had given me quite a bit of notoriety. But the carabiniere, who either wasn't alive then or had been just a child, had never heard of the show or of me. He smiled uncomfortably, and with the authority he now had, which Nadar and I have both lacked for a while, said patiently, Back to the matter at hand.

I was embarrassed—normally I'm a man who measures his

words, without rigmarole—and I repeated that thieves had destroyed our apartment. But again I lost control and went on confusedly about the delivery girl who wanted five extra euros, and the man who'd hoodwinked me the week before, right under our building. Not only that: I pulled in Nadar, pressing him to talk about the girl who'd buzzed our intercom various times during the week, and the couple that had shown up just the night before. He was happy to take over, listing every buzz of the intercom, running back over a great many negligible details. He stopped himself only when the door behind us opened, and before the three of us turned around, someone motioned to the carabiniere. The boy burst out laughing. He struggled to pull himself together, muttering an apology, and in the end he asked:

—What did they steal from you?

—What did they steal from us? I repeated, though addressing my wife. And she, who had remained silent this whole time, said quietly,

—Nothing.

—Gold? asked the carabiniere.

—I only have these earrings, but I always wear them.

—You don't have other jewels?

—A string of pearls that belonged to my mother, but they didn't find it.

—Was it well hidden?

—No.

I stepped in:

The thieves upended everything but without rhyme or reason, they didn't even find the fifty euros that my wife had stashed in the kitchen cupboard. The money ended up under a container of detergent they'd overturned, out of spite.

The young man assumed a disgruntled expression, and then he started talking chiefly to Nadar. They're gypsies, he said, kids who get in through the windows and balconies.

They pile furniture against the door in case the owners come back, and they start rummaging everywhere. They look for gold, ladies and gentlemen, and if they don't find any they get their revenge by demolishing everything. I clarified that there was no furniture against the door, that the door hadn't opened easily because of the all the debris stuck under it. Then I added, Maybe you should send someone to have a look, say, for fingerprints. At this point the carabiniere grew less patient. He made it clear, in a firm tone, with the diction of a well-educated boy, that TV was one thing and realty another, that things of this kind happened all the time, that we were lucky not to have been murdered in our sleep. He said that the government was cutting back the police force and beefing up the army, something that, in a phase of increasing hardship, was detrimental for the safety of citizens and, possibly, even for democracy. He made it clear that being a judge in the past, talking on TV in the past, only proved that if today's world was such a mess it was also our responsibility. He advised us, in the end, to put bars on the windows and resort to an alarm system that would immediately signal any infraction to the nearest police car on duty. Even if, he added with unmasked irony, I don't see the point, given that you have nothing to steal.

My wife fretted in her seat:

—The cat's missing.

—Ah.

—What if they've taken him?

—Why would they?

—I don't know, to ask for a ransom?

The carabiniere smiled at her with a warmth he hadn't conveyed either to me or to Nadar. Anything is possible, Signora Minori, he said. But now banish upsetting thoughts from your mind and focus on the positive: this is a great opportunity to reorganize your apartment, get rid of what you don't need, rediscover useful things you'd forgotten about. As for the cat, maybe he took advantage of the situation to go looking for girl-friends.

I laughed, so did Nadar.

Vanda didn't.

7.

We went back home. It was no longer raining. It took some effort to rid ourselves of our neighbor, who wanted to come up and check out the disaster in person. He's an old fool, my wife said, getting angry. He bored the carabiniere with his bragging, and you weren't any better. I didn't object. It was depressing to admit, but she was right. I helped her to at least straighten up the kitchen a bit, but she soon sent me away. I only complicated her job. I withdrew to the balcony off my study. I hoped, after so much rain, that the air would have cooled down, but it was still sultry, with foul, bothersome drops that wet my hair, my shirt.

Vanda called me to dinner, perhaps a bit too loftily. We didn't say much. At a certain point she again brought up the idea of calling the children, and I objected, saying they already led complicated lives, better to leave them in peace, at least while they were on vacation. Sandro must have only just arrived at his in-laws' in Provence, and Anna was most likely on Crete with some new boyfriend. Let's not disturb them, I said, trying to protect them, but she wanted to send a message to both anyway, something along the lines of: We had a break-in and we can't find Labes. Anna responded immediately, in her usual, truncated way: Oh God, poor you, sorry, don't wear yourselves out; while Sandro, also in his fashion, got back to us an hour later with an extremely detailed text. He'd been at our place the night before, as agreed. He'd stayed from nine to nine thirty. He told us to tell the police that at that hour the house was in perfect condition, and Labes in excellent health. He wrapped up with affectionate words suggesting that we go to a hotel at least for the first night.

Vanda was more comforted by the messages from her children than by my presence, which seemed to be getting increasingly on her nerves. After dinner we turned to straightening up the bedroom, and I suddenly remembered the story about the taxi driver and my wife's reaction. I was gripped by the fear that, in the chaos of misplaced objects, she'd stumble upon something of mine that might sadden or offend her. As soon as the bed was minimally useable, I convinced her to lie down.

—And you?

—I'll deal with the living room for a while.

—Don't bang around.

I went straightaway to check if the heavy metal cube that I'd bought many decades ago in Prague was still in its place, at the top of the shelves in my study. It was the same object that had caught the attention of the solenoid girl, an object lacquered in blue, twenty centimeters wide, twenty high. Vanda had never liked it, but it meant something to me. When we'd moved into this house, I'd taken it upon myself, after a lengthy quarrel, to position it high up, along with other decorative objects that we didn't particularly care for. Apparently to satisfy my wife, I'd pushed it far back, so that one saw little or no part of it from below. In truth I wanted her, over time, to forget about it. Vanda didn't know that you just needed to firmly press the middle of one of the facets so that it opened like a door. She also didn't know, naturally, that this was the object's feature that had inspired me to buy it; I wanted to protect my secrets inside. I ascertained with relief that, although it now hovered dangerously over the edge, it had remained in its place.

8.

I carefully closed the doors that separate the living room and the study from the bedroom. The fresh scent of rain and basil was finally drifting in through the open balcony doors. Now that Vanda slept, and I no longer felt obliged to reassure her, anxiety quickly took hold of me. As of late every little worry becomes an obsession, entering my head and growing out of proportion. I can't drive it out. In that moment, I sensed that the man who'd taken one hundred euros from me, and the woman who'd nabbed five, were about to have their turn. It suddenly occurred to me that the two could have been in on it together, that together they'd organized the invasion of my house or, more simply, that they'd sold my address to thieves. The hypothesis seemed increasingly sound, and the next thing I knew, the couple that, according to Nadar, had buzzed our intercom assumed their faces. I imagined them dissatisfied after the first round, I thought that maybe they'd already decided to send in other people, more skilled, or to come back themselves. I won't go to bed, I told myself, I'll wait up for them.

Me? Wait for them? And to confront them how, with what strength, what determination?

The years were beginning to weigh on me. Not only had I learned that I ran the risk of mistaking two stairs for one and falling, that my hearing was worse than Nadar's, that I could no longer count on my reflexes when facing any kind of urgency or danger. There was more. I would convince myself, let's say, that I'd just taken some medication, that I'd turned off the gas or the faucet, but actually I'd only thought about doing it. I'd confuse a moment in a dream from God knows how long ago for something that had really happened. More and more often, while reading, I'd mangle words, so much so that recently I'd had a lapse in front of a printed page fixed to doorway. It appeared to say LEGAL SUICIDE THIS WAY, when it actually said LEGAL STUDIO THIS WAY. As for the past few days, it was clear that people perceived, more clearly than I did, the unraveling of my defenses, and took advantage of it. Which was why I felt ridiculous. I said to myself, you're old, you're delirious, straighten things up a bit and go to bed. But I didn't know where to start. I scouted out my study and the living room. In the end I decided to move everything to be tossed out into to the foyer. I checked the status of the two computers which, miraculously, still worked, while various devices for watching films and listening to music no longer did. I pushed away, with a broom, what was scattered on the floor—books, shards of vases and knickknacks, old photographs, old VHS tapes, records, countless notepads of Vanda's, CDs and DVDs, papers, documents, various objects, in brief, what the thieves had overturned from the loft space, the drawers, the shelves—to the edges of the two rooms.

It was hard work, and when I was done I examined the slightly cleared spaces with satisfaction. At that point I decided to move on to sort through the materials in my study. I sat on the floor, letting out a groan or two, and I heaped together the shards with the shards, the books with the books, the papers with the papers and so on. At the start I worked swiftly. I was grieved that several books had been split in two, that they'd lost their covers, that they were in tatters. Anyway, I carried on, setting the books that were in good shape to one side, the ruined ones to another. But then I made the mistake of leafing through one of them and almost against my will, I started to read passages that, who knows when, I'd underlined. I was intrigued. Why had I circled certain words? What had prompted me to put exclamation points next to a passage that I now found, in rereading, insignificant? I forgot that I was putting things back in order so that Vanda wouldn't get depressed when she woke up. I forgot that I was there, in essence, because I wasn't sleepy, because it was hot, because I didn't feel safe, because I was afraid the thieves would return, that they would threaten us, that they would tie us to the bed and beat us. Instead I was engrossed by what I'd underlined. I read entire pages, struggling to recall the year I'd devoted to this book or that (1958, 1960, 1962, before marriage, after?). It wasn't the written conscience of the authors I was chasing after—they were often names I'd forgotten, aging pages, concepts by now no longer used in contemporary culture—but rather, my own conscience: What had seemed right to me in the past, my convictions, my thoughts, my Self in the making.

The night was perfectly silent. Naturally I wasn't able to find myself in any of that scrawling, in any of the exclamation points (what happens to the lovely sentences that enter our minds, how do they rouse us, how do they become devoid of meaning, or unrecognizable, or embarrassing, or ridiculous?), and I ended up forgetting the books. I proceeded to replace, into boxes and folders, papers of various sizes, index cards of my reading, notebooks with novels and short stories written before I'd turned twenty, countless cuttings from newspapers of the articles I'd published, also those in which others talked about me. To that huge amount of paper I added reels of radio programs, cassettes and DVDs that showed me on television in my glory days, all the things that Vanda diligently saved, without ever showing any particular interest in what I did. And here it was, I'd dug up a great many things that attested to how I'd spent a rather long life. Was I that stuff? Was I the scrawls on the books I'd read, was I the sheets of paper crammed with titles and quotes (for example this: "Our cities are the breeding grounds of livestock; families, schools, churches are slaughterhouses for children; colleges and universities are the kitchens. As adults, in marriage and in business, we consume the finished product"; and also: "The appearance of love is the subverter of every decent social order of our lives")? Was I a long wordy novel written at twenty about a boy who had to slave night and day to pay his father his weight in gold, thereby unshackling himself from him and from his family of origin? Was I the paragraphs on the chemists' contract I'd published in the mid-seventies, was I the comments on the party platform, was I the reviews of books that talked about the worker on the assembly line, was I amusing clips on daily life in a big city—traffic, exasperating lines at the bank or in the post office—was I the ironic observations that had given me a little fame and, step by step, transformed me into a television writer of some success? Was I the thoughtful interviews I granted to this one or the other, was I the harsh criticism of so and so and the praise from such and such for what I'd invented for TV in the eighties and nineties? Was I my body moving in the corner of a simulated terrace, under lights that replicated broad daylight? Was I my voice thirty years ago, conversational, cordial, arrogant? I remembered how much I'd toiled since the sixties, hard labor—as they say—to realize my potential. Was this the fulfillment of it? A concrete accumulation, through the decades, of papers, handwritten, printed, a trail of scrawls, reports, pages, newspapers, floppy discs, USB fobs, hard disks, the cloud? My potential realized, Myself made real: that is to say, a chaos that could overflow, if I just typed Aldo Minori, from the living room to the Google archives?

I imposed a rule: stop reading and skimming. I went back to the work of sorting. I put back, into cardboard boxes, Vanda's countless notepads: figure upon figure, a punctilious financial account of our family from 1962 to today, sheets of graph paper on which she'd noted in detail the incoming and outgoing sums that maybe, were she to agree, needed at this point to be tossed. I piled up the books I wanted to unload in the middle of the room and I sloppily arranged those in decent shape on the shelves that hadn't been dismantled. I placed the folders with newspaper clippings, the boxes of notebooks, the ones full of VHS tapes and DVDs on the table. I put the shards that I managed to gather up in a garbage bag, tearing it in various places, and so I put it into another. Last but not least I started to gather up the photographs, images of the distant past along with those more recent.

I hadn't looked at old photographs for a long time, I found them ugly and uninteresting. I was used to digital pictures by now, Vanda and I had tons of them on the computer: image after image of mountains, fields, butterflies, roses in bloom or just about to open, seasides, cities, monuments, paintings, sculptures, and then relatives, the exes of our children, the new boyfriends and girlfriends, our grandchildren captured in every phase of development, the children who were friends with our grandchildren. Life, in short, never so copiously documented. The present, the present perfect: better to leave the remote past alone.

I avoided looking at myself. I didn't like myself as an old man, and I'd never liked myself when I was younger. Instead I glanced at Sandro and Anna when they were little. They were so lovely. I saw the boyfriends and girlfriends they'd had when they were teenagers, likeable young people who'd quickly disappeared. I found friends of mine and of Vanda's whom we'd forgotten, people we'd seen steadily, only to no longer remember their first names, or to call them cattily by last names. I paused to study a photo taken in our courtyard, who knows who took it, maybe Sandro. It dated back to the first years we'd lived in this house. Along with me and Vanda there was Nadar, who back then—I calculated—must have already been over sixty, though if one were to compare him to how he was now, he seemed young. We change so much, even in advanced age, I thought to myself, staring at him for a moment. Our neighbor, in the picture, was tall, pleasant-looking, still with some hair on his head. I was about to set it aside when I was struck by Vanda. For a fraction of a second, astonished, I thought I didn't recognize her. How old was she then, fifty, forty-five? I lingered over other pictures of her, especially the ones in black-and-white. The feeling of looking at a stranger solidified. I'd met her in 1960, I was twenty, she was twenty-two. Little or nothing had stayed with me from those years. I couldn't recall if I'd ever found her beautiful. Back then beauty was a vulgar notion to me. Safe to say I liked her. I thought she was graceful, I desired her to a reasonable degree. She was a clever girl, watchful. I fell in love with her for those qualities, and also because it seemed incredible that, in spite of having so many virtues, she'd fallen in love with me. Two years later we were married, and she'd become the meticulous organizer of our day-to-day life, one involving study and occasional work, no money, always scrimping and saving.

I recognized the features of that period: flimsy clothes she sewed herself, scuffed shoes with worn-out heels, no makeup on her large eyes. What I didn't recognize, on the other hand, was her youth. This, then, was what was alien to me: her youth. In those pictures Vanda radiated a glow which—I discovered—I had no memory of, not even a spark that allowed me to say: Yes, she used to be like this. I thought of the person who now slept in the bedroom, the person who had been my wife for fifty years. It wasn't clear to me that she'd really been the way she appeared in those photos. Why? Had I barely looked at her from the very start? How much of her had I relegated to the corner of my eye without noticing? I fished out all her old pictures from 1960 to 1974. I stopped at that meaningful year for us: there were't many, one didn't take so many pictures back then. They were proof of a woman who, up until her forties, had been attractive, perhaps even beautiful. I examined a picture in reddish hues on the back of which was written, in pencil: 1973. It showed Vanda with Sandro, who was eight years old at the time, and Anna, who was four. The children seemed happy, pressed against their mother, who in turn seemed pleased, and all three looked at me, delighted, as I took the picture. Their cheerful gaze marked my presence, proving that in that moment I, too, was there. And yet only now did I realize that my wife was bursting with a joie de vivre that rendered her dazzling. I closed up the pictures quickly in a couple of metal boxes. Everything lost through carelessness. Had I really never paid attention to Vanda? And in any case, what did that question even mean, given there was no way now to verify anything? In the bedroom, only the green irises below heavy lids remained as they'd been five decades ago.

I got up, I looked at my watch. It was ten past three, and I could hear only the call of some nocturnal bird. I closed the window, lowered the shades, reexamined the study. There was still a lot to do, but it was getting better. And I was about to go to bed, when I spotted a large fragment of a flower vase that had escaped my notice. I picked it up and underneath I found a yellow envelope, swollen and bound by an elastic. I recognized it at once even though I hadn't thought about it for decades, even though I'd buried it God knows where precisely so that I would never think of it again. It contained the letters that Vanda had written to me between 1974 and 1978.

I felt irked, embarrassed, contrite, and I thought of hiding the envelope before my wife woke up. Or putting it among the papers to toss out and going immediately, now, to the dumpster. The letters harbored the traces of a pain so intense that, if freed, it could have crossed the study, spread through the living room, burst through the closed doors and returned to take possession of Vanda, shaking her, yanking her out of sleep, prompting her to rant and rave at the top of her lungs. But I didn't hide the envelope, nor did I toss it into the trash. As if flattened by a weight that suddenly came back, bearing down on my shoulders, I sat back down on the floor. I pulled away the elastic and after almost forty years I read, though out of order, a few of the aging pages, ten lines here, fifteen there.

CHAPTER TWO

1.

In case it's slipped your mind, Dear Sir, let me remind you: I am your wife. These were the first words my eyes landed on that night, instantly taking me back to when I left home because I'd fallen in love with another woman. At the top of the letter was the date: April 30th, 1974. The past, very remote. A mild morning in Naples in the drab apartment we'd had back then. In love. Maybe that's what I should have said: Vanda, I've fallen in love. Instead I expressed myself in a more brutal and, come to think of it now, less definitive way.

The fitful shadows of the children weren't there in the apartment. Sandro was at school, Anna at daycare. I said, Vanda, I have something to confess, I've been with another woman. She stared at me, stunned, and I myself was terrified by those words. I muttered: I could have hidden it but I wanted to tell you the truth. And I added, I'm sorry, it happened, it's small-minded to repress desire.

Vanda insulted me, she cried, she struck my chest with clenched fists. She apologized, she got mad again. I'd assumed, of course, that she was not going to take it well, but such a violent reaction surprised me. She was a good-natured woman, reasonable, and so I struggled to register that she would not be easily appeased. It didn't matter to her that the institution of marriage was in crisis, that the family was in its death throes, that fidelity was a virtue of the petty bourgeoisie. She wanted our marriage to be a miraculous exception. She wanted our family to be healthy. She wanted us, always, to be faithful to one another. And as a result she despaired, she demanded that I reveal right away the woman with whom I'd betrayed her. Betrayed, yes, she screamed at me at a certain point, and humiliated her.

In the evening, choosing my words carefully, I tried to explain that it wasn't a matter of betrayal, that I had enormous respect for her, that real betrayal was when you betrayed your own instinct, your needs, your body, yourself. Bullshit, she shrieked, but then immediately she contained herself so as not to wake the children. We fought all night with lowered voices, and her unscreaming pain, a pain that enlarged her eyes and distorted her features, terrorized me even more than the screaming version. It terrorized me without involving me; her torment never entered my heart as if it were my own. I was in a state of intoxication that cloaked me as if it were a fire-proof suit. I withdrew, taking my time. I said I thought it was important that she understood. I said we both needed to think, that I was confused and that she needed to help me. Then I cleared out and didn't go home for several days.

2.

I don't know what I had in mind, maybe nothing in particular. I certainly didn't hate my wife, I hadn't built up any resentment toward her, I loved her. I'd thought it was pleasantly adventurous to get married when I was so young, before graduating, without a job. I'd felt I was cutting away my father's hold over me and that I was finally in charge of my own life. Of course the undertaking was risky, the sources of income I could count on were precarious, and at times I was afraid. But the first years were wonderful, we'd felt like a new kind of couple, battling the existing order. Then the adventure transformed, little by little, into a routine imposed upon us by the needs of the children. What had suddenly changed, above all, was the backdrop against which I was playing the role of the husband and father. Now everything around us seemed struck by decline. A plague revealed itself in every institution, starting with the university, where I'd started to work without prospects. Being married, having a family at a young age, was no longer a sign of autonomy, but of being behind the times. I was still in my twenties and yet I felt old and—in spite of myself—part of a world, a lifestyle that, in the political and cultural environment I'd latched onto, was considered finished. And so, soon, even though I had a sound relationship with my wife and kids, I succumbed to the lure of habits that programmatically cut away all traditional bonds. Once, with the excuse that my ring finger had thickened, I had my wedding band cut off. Vanda was upset about it, she waited for me to put on another ring. I did nothing. She continued wearing her wedding band.

It's likely that the relationship with Lidia—she'd just enrolled in economics and business, in keeping with the fashion of the era, and I was a lecturer of Greek grammar without a future—was encouraged by that climate, fueled by it. Surely I must have thought that renouncing her to avoid wronging my wife and children was a sort of anachronism. And seeing each other in secret, according to the established pattern of clandestine relationships, also seemed contrary to the spirit of the times. Lidia wasn't yet twenty years old but she already had a job and her own place on a pretty, fragrant street. Ringing her bell whenever I could, taking walks with her, going together to the cinema or the theater, were such urgent needs that they prompted me to spill the beans almost immediately with Vanda. But I didn't think the desire would have taken root, that I would have wanted that girl again and again. Rather, I was more or less certain that the impetus to be with her would soon ebb, that Lidia herself would cool off in order to go back to the young guy she'd been seeing for a few months, or because she'd found someone else, someone her own age, free and childless. As a result, in revealing my affair to Vanda, I only wanted the time to enjoy it unharrassed, without subterfuge, until it had run its course. In other words, when I left the house, after that first fight, I didn't doubt for a minute that I'd soon be back. I told myself: This pause serves *also* to recast my relationship with my wife, to make clear that we need to go beyond the norms of cohabitation that have kept us together so far. And this, perhaps, was the motivation for my saying to her *I've been with another woman* rather than *I'm in love with another woman*.

Falling in love, in those days, had become a somewhat ridiculous notion, a vestige of the past century, indicating a dangerous tendency to conglomerate; if it began to surface, you immediately had to fight against it so as not to generate distress in one's partner. Being with another woman, on the other hand, assumed an increased legitimacy, whether married or not. *I'd been with another woman, I was with another woman, I'm with another woman* were sentences that expressed liberty, not guilt. I realized, of course, that to a wife's ears the formula might sound atrocious, especially to Vanda who, like me, was raised with the idea that *first* one fell in love with someone and *then*, with that someone, one stayed. But—I thought—she has to accept that it can happen, that it's happened, that perhaps, when I go back to the family, it will happen again. And looking at it this way—hoping that Vanda understood, that she would adjust to present times and not create further scenes—I spent happy days, ever happier, with Lidia.

I realized late that it wasn't just about a sexual give and take, or a key piece in the battle against the very concept of adultery, or a joyful erotic friendship, or one of the various liberating practices that were recasting the world. I loved that girl. I loved her in the most old-fashioned way, that is to say, utterly. The idea of leaving her, going back to my wife and children, abandoning her to others, took away my will to live.

3.

It took me a year to admit it to myself, albeit still with some reticence. But I never had the strength to tell Vanda, which made me all the more responsible for her deterioration. At first the fact that I'd been with another woman seemed terrible to her. Then, absorbing the blow as best she could, she tried to consider the matter a momentary yielding owed to my meager experience of women, and thus to my sexual curiosity. She hoped that after a few days the fever would pass, and so she took it upon herself, out loud and in writing, to cure me. She seemed in a daze. She couldn't believe that she—she who had put me at the center of her life, who'd slept with me for years, who'd given me two children, who'd seen to my every need in an exemplary manner—had been set aside for an unknown woman who would never be able to take care of me in that same devoted way.

Every time we met—often after long absences on my part—she tried to put forth, calmly and clearly, all the questions she'd pondered over. We would sit at the kitchen table and she would try to list the practical problems caused by my disappearances, the fact that the kids needed me, the reasons for her bewilderment. Her tone was generally polite, but one morning she snapped.

—Did I do something wrong? she asked me.

—Absolutely not.

—Then what is it that's not working?

—Nothing, it's a complicated time, that's all.

—You think it's complicated beacause you fail to see me.

—I see you.

—No, you only see the woman who sweats over the stove, who keeps the house clean, who takes care of the kids. But I'm something else, I'm a person.

Person, person, person, she started to scream, and then struggled to calm down again. They were long, difficult hours. In that phase she tried to show me that she hadn't stood still for the past ten years, that she had matured, that she was a new woman. She did this while wringing her hands to contain her distress, saying: Is it possible that you, only you, weren't aware of it? And if I, who didn't know how to respond to her, strayed from the point, cataloging the evils of the family and the need to liberate oneself, she came down to my level, she indicated with forced politeness that the books I read were ones she was familiar with, that she, too, had been working for some time on her own liberation, that we could, should, have been doing this work together. Then, at a certain point—since she could see from my face that I couldn't wait to leave in order to protect my state of grace from her painful existence, and from the anxiety that her spectacle of suffering provoked—the politeness gave way and the tenor of our meetings changed. Vanda would begin, scornfully, then she'd start screaming, she'd burst into tears, insulting me. Once she screamed out of the blue:

—Am I boring you? Tell me that I bore you.

—No.

—Then why are you always looking at your watch? Are you in a hurry, are you afraid of missing a train?

—I drove here.

—Her car?

—Yes.

—Is she waiting for you? What are you doing tonight? Going out to a restaurant?

She started to laugh for no reason. She went into the bedroom, singing old children's songs at the top of her voice.

After a while, of course, she got a grip, she always got a grip. But every time she did I felt she'd lost some part of herself that, in the past, had attracted me. It had never been like this, she was ruining herself because of me. And yet I considered that self-ruin to be the authorization to distance myself from her even further. Is it possible, I wondered, that gaining a little freedom has to be so hard? Why are we such a backward country? Why, in more evolved nations, does everything happen without histrionics?

On one occasion I was about to leave. It was late afternoon on a very hot day. She ran to the door and locked it. She called Sandro and Anna and said: Dad feels like he's in prison, so let's play prison for real. The kids pretended to enjoy it, I pretended with them, but not her, she was saying softly: Ha ha, now you don't get out anymore. Then she threw the keys at me and locked herself in the bathroom. I didn't dare leave, I sent Sandro to call her. She reemerged, she said, I was kidding. But she wasn't kidding at all. She was tired, she no longer slept, she was trying to figure out how to talk sense into me. Since she was getting nowhere she tried now to rouse me, now to anger me, now to beg me, now to scare me. You shouldn't keep me here this way, I told her. She responded, indignant: Who's keeping you, get out. But two seconds later she said quietly: Wait, sit, your madness is driving me mad.

What exasperated her, what wore her down, was that I didn't want to explain why I'd done what I'd done. She asked me, she wrote me, *why*. But I didn't know what to tell her. I invented convoluted replies, at times I muttered: I don't know. I was lying of course, by then I knew the reason, I knew it with growing clarity. The time with Lidia was joyful time, carefree time, I could never get enough. I felt full of energy, I was writing, publishing. People liked me. It was as if the swamp that I'd carried inside since childhood, that had lasted until a short while ago, had suddenly been reclaimed by that cheerful and elegant woman. In the beginning that April had been marvelous: sleeping with her in spring, eating with her in spring, walking with her in spring, traveling with her in spring. And looking at her—looking at her, enchanted—while she put on and took off her springtime clothes. I'd thought: I'll go back home at the end of May. But spring slipped away and when the last day of the season came I felt I was dying. And so I said to myself, let's wait for summer, I still want to have Lidia all summer. But summer too passed and I didn't know how I would stand autumn without her. Then, in turn, autumn went by, winter went by, and that whole year, despite the visits with my wife and children, nothing counted except Spring Lidia, Summer Lidia, Autumn Lidia, Winter Lidia. That is to say, the coveted time was hers; I was afraid of the time with Vanda, with Sandro and Anna. I pushed it back, I whittled it to a minimum with one excuse after another. When I was with them I protected myself by lying, and the deception served to protect the extraordinary sense of well-being that had taken hold of me. In those moments I felt humiliated both by my incapacity to be true and by the unbearable truth of my wife's desperation, by the disorientation of the children. To be as I felt, to really say *why* I was behaving that way, I would have had to speak of my happiness with Lidia. But what could have been more cruel? Vanda wanted something else. Vanda, so as to rise above her desperation, expected me to tell her: I realize I've made a mistake, let's get back together. This was the dead end.

4.

We didn't pull out of it that year, nor the following. My wife grew thin, squandering her vitality, losing even more control of herself. By now she was like a person suspended in a void, and her panic contributed considerably to depleting her remaining strength.

In the beginning I believed that the terrible situation we'd ended up in concerned only the two of us, not Sandro and Anna. And, in fact, I've now seen the children in my mind's eye: They're blurry figures, they don't have our clear contours as we argue and fight in the kitchen; we're well-defined in spite of the time that's passed. Sandro and Anna aren't in my head, or if they are, they're doing something else, playing or watching television. Our crisis, the anguish that devours us, is elsewhere, it doesn't involve them. But then, at a certain point, things changed. During a fight, Vanda, burst out that I had to tell her whether I still wanted to take care of the children or if I intended to get rid of them the way I was getting rid of her. I was flabbergasted. Of course I want to take care of them, I replied. Good to know, she said quietly, and dropped the question. But as she realized that time was passing and that I was alternating long absences with brief appearances, she told me that if I didn't want to account for what I had done to her, I had to account for what I'd done to the children. How would I put it to them?

I hadn't thought about it. The children, prior to that disaster, constituted a fact of existence. They'd been born and now they were there. In my free time I played with them, I took them out, I invented fairy tales for them. I praised them, I reproached them. But in general, after amusing them sufficiently, or after rebuking them with benevolent authority, I holed up to study, and my wife entertained them with great imagination, dedicating herself to housework all the while. I never saw anything wrong with the way things were going, and Vanda herself never complained, even when we were besieged by that culture of deinstitutionalization—what an ugly word— of everything. We were both raised to believe that things were naturally supposed to be a certain way. It was natural that our marriage should last until death separated us. It was natural that my wife should have no job other than housework. And even now that everything seemed to be in transition—a pre-Revolutionary phase, people said—it was inconceivable that mothers would stop taking care of their children. Now she was the one raising the issue, asking how I planned to deal with it. Yet again I didn't know what to tell her. We were on the street, in Piazza Municipio. She stopped, locking eyes with me, and asked:

—Do you want to continue being a father?

—Yes.

—And how? By showing up once or twice to twist the knife in the wound, then staying away for months? Having kids on demand, only when it's convenient for you?

—I'll come see them every weekend.

—Oh, *you'll come see them*. You mean they're staying with me?

I grew confused, I stammered:

—Well, I can take them for a while, as well.

—As well? As well?—she screamed. I take them *always*, and you take them *as well*? You want to destroy them the way you're destroying me? Children don't need parents *as well*, but *always*.

She ran off, ditching me a few yards from the city hall.

I forced myself to come back to Naples every weekend. I left Rome, I went to the house where we'd lived for a dozen years. My plan was to avoid fighting with Vanda. I couldn't take it anymore, and she, too, was shaken—she lit one cigarette after another with unsteady hands, she had the eyes of someone who sees no way out. To avoid her, I closed myself up in a room with the kids. I soon discovered that it was impossible. Though the spaces of the house were the same, neither I nor my children were able to be together with the same nonchalance. Everything was false now. I felt obligated to spend my time with them, happily, and they—they weren't the same anymore. They threw me anxious looks, attuned to what their mother and I did and said. They were afraid of making a mistake, of upsetting me, thus losing me forever. They felt obligated to spend time happily with me. But in spite of willing it with all our might, in no way were we able—father and children—to behave naturally. Vanda was in the other room, and the three of us knew not to forget her. She was so much a part of us that withdrawing was a useless effort. She left us alone for a long time, this was true. She didn't interfere. But we heard the noises of her toiling, or a nervous humming. We should have ignored her, learned to be just us three, regroup beyond the old quartet. But we weren't able to, we felt her presence as a threat—not that she wanted to harm us. We feared, rather, the threat of her suffering—and we felt that not a movement or a word of ours was lost on her, that whenever a chair or a table creaked, she suffered. Time, therefore, tended to dilate unbearably; evening never came. After a while I didn't know what to come up with. I distracted myself, I thought of Lidia. It was Saturday. Maybe she'd gone to the movies with friends, what did I know? I planned to say out loud: I'm going down for cigarettes, and to look for a phone, to call her before she went out, before the device rang on and on leaving me with a sense of abandonment. Vanda seemed particularly sensitive to those distractions. All of a sudden she peeped out. She read it in my face, she intuited the burden of staying with my children. I had never been there this long in normal times. Never like this, in any case: It was almost like taking an exam which my wife, their mother, had the authority to grade.

At times she couldn't contain herself.

—How's it going?

—Fine.

—You're not playing?

—We are playing.

—What?

—Crazy Heights.

—Kids, let Dad win, if not he gets upset.

—She was never satisfied. She scolded me for turning on the TV, she criticized me for playing violent games, she told me derisively that I overstimulated the kids and that they wouldn't be able to get to sleep. The tension became intolerable, and we'd end up fighting in front of Sandro and Anna. The scenes were no longer monitored. Vanda convinced herself that the kids should know, evaluate, judge.

—Lower your voice, please.

—Why? Are you afraid they'll know who you really are?

—Not at all.

—You want to do to them what you did to me? Do they have to believe that you love them when it's not true?

—I've always loved you, I still do.

—Don't lie to me. Don't tell me lies I can't stand anymore. Not in front of the kids. If you have to lie, then get out of here.

Sandro and Anna had quickly learned that each of my appearances entailed the unchecked pain of their mother. So if perhaps, in the beginning, they waited for the pleasure of seeing me again and hoped that I would always stay, later they started to pretend to focus on their own games or shows on TV, wishing meanwhile that I would get out before the storm broke. The fact is, I myself tended to shorten my visits, to duck out as soon as I sensed that Vanda was about to crack. Once I brought some gifts for the children, a sweater for Sandro, a little necklace for Anna. When she realized her daughter was happy she said:

—You bought this stuff?

—Yes, who do you think bought it?

—Lidia.

—What are you talking about?

—You're turning red, it was her.

—It's not true.

—You need help buying your children a present? Don't you dare give them something that comes from her, ever again.

In fact it really had been Lidia, but that wasn't the point. Every scene that Vanda made in that phase had an ulterior motive. She wanted to demonstrate—not only to me but most of all to herself—that I couldn't be a father without her, that I didn't know how. That by excluding her I excluded myself, and that without a reconciliation, life—namely, the way we'd lived until the moment I'd confessed my betrayal—was no longer possible.

This thesis soon seemed solid to me. Turning up every Saturday, every Sunday; seeing Sandro and Anna, who welcomed me, cleaned up, hair combed, as if for a stranger's visit; sensing those first affectionate minutes charged with an excessive tension for them and for me. All this seemed not only useless but dangerous. My presence in the house was meant to give continuity to the idea of a father figure, but because it wasn't permanent, it was necessarily flawed. Whatever I did or said seemed, to Vanda, insufficient. She demonstrated to me point by point—with the rigorous logic that she was always capable of and that had now intensified—that I didn't give adequate replies to the mute demands of our children, that I was letting them down.

—What do they expect? I asked her one morning, more scared than ever.

—To understand, she shouted at me with a voice that cracked in her chest and seemed to suffocate her. To understand why you went away to live somewhere else, why you abandoned them, why you're only with them halfheartedly a few hours before going off, without making clear when you'll be back, or when you'll give them what they deserve.

I told her she was right, in part to calm her, in part because I didn't know how to object. What kind of father was I, what kind of father could I have been, in that house where, for years, we'd had the absolute certainty that we would have lived, the four of us, forever? The architecture had absorbed our way of being together, assigning corners for every function. And though the spaces were gloomy, cold in winter, too hot in summer, never bright, they had nevertheless conformed to loving habits, often with peaks of bliss. Living in the house for a few hours a week based on the new situation was impossible for me. And so one day, at the height of the usual quarrel, I said to Vanda:

—School's closed, I'll keep the kids with me for a bit.

—With you how?

—With me.

—You want to take them away from me?

—No, what are you talking about?

—You want to take them away from me, she said, morose.

But then she agreed. She agreed in a dramatic way, as if it were a matter of a final, definitive experiment, after which she would understand exactly what I had in mind.

5.

I took the kids to Rome one Sunday in summer, and they seemed happy. But it was a stupid thing to do. I didn't have my own place—I couldn't afford it—and on the other hand I didn't feel like keeping them at Lidia's. The reasons were, as usual, difficult to unravel. I predicted that if she hosted all three of us in her studio apartment and Vanda found out about it, she would have seen, in that choice, a sort of cancellation of her, as if to say: Get out of the way, you're no longer needed, neither as a mother nor as a wife. She was increasingly dominated by a pressing logic that impeded every arbitration, and I feared that the abstract series of dots she connected could push her—it was already pushing her every day—she was always physically weaker, mentally more alert—to extremes that I didn't even want to consider. But her reaction wasn't the only thing that worried me. Being observed by the children when I was with Lidia, in her bright house, at breakfast, at lunch, at dinner, in her bed, was loathsome to me. It was saying in effect to Sandro, to Anna: Look at this girl, see how well-behaved she is, how calm, how well we get along; I live here, do you like it? And I intuited that, in doing so, I would have coerced them, for the sake of my love, into a cohabitation that—especially if they were to agree that Lidia was indeed nice—would have been an insult to their love for their mother. Not just that, there was more. I didn't want Lidia to see me in the role of a father. Living with her and the two kids for days, occupying her tiny space, making a mess, showing her my responsibility, forcing her to share it with me, seemed unacceptable. Until a short while ago, thanks to the labors of Vanda, I didn't realize I'd had any—none that were onerous, at any rate. I didn't want to show Lidia, in all its concreteness, what I was: a thirty-six year old man, rigidly defined, married, the father of two children, eleven and seven years old. Inside that magical space, I didn't even want to see myself that way. There I felt a lover, uninhibited, one who doesn't free oneself only to be tied down again. I was casting a new mold for love affairs. I didn't want to be a person who dragged, into the house of a young woman whose future was ahead of her, the legacy of his dreary past.

I stayed with a friend. I knew nothing about caring for children, and I quickly let the wife deal with it. Both were on my side, they supported me. They said, though they were a happy couple, stably married for five years, that one couldn't, one shouldn't resist impulses, that I was right to give in to my passions, and that I should stop feeling guilty. One evening, while the children slept, the husband and wife gave me a judicious scolding because I never denigrated my wife.

—Why should I? I asked.

—Because she's going overboard, people shouldn't act this way, my friend said.

—I'm hurting her deeply, she reacts the best she can.

—She reacts in a very unpleasant way, exclaimed the wife.

—It's hard to suffer politely.

—Others do. Composure, in certain cases, is everything.

—Maybe the people you know don't suffer as much as Vanda.

I defended her earnestly, but they kept saying that I was the nicer one, the more composed. And so when Sandro and Anna would go to bed, and I was sure that they were sleeping, I'd leave them under the affectionate watch of my hosts and run to Lidia. Every hour I spent with her, ever since the beginning of our relationship, surprised me. Those hours were so distant from the hardship I was used to with Vanda. Lidia was bought up to live well, it came to her naturally. She valued comfort and pleasure, she went to lengths to welcome me, cheerfully. She shared her small earnings with me if I was in a tight spot. She took our complicated situation in stride without fretting about the future. I was happy when she opened the door and the table was set for a late, sumptuous dinner; I was unhappy when I had to leave her bed before dawn. I'd come back at five-thirty in the morning to the kids, hoping they hadn't woken up. I'd roam around the house without feeling sleepy, filled with a sense of guilt. I would often sit next to Sandro and Anna's bed, watching them, trying to absorb them, to feel that they were indispensable to me. I'd wake them up a few hours later. I'd wait for them to have breakfast, to wash up, and then, given that my friend and his wife had their affairs to tend to, I would drag them to work with me.

Sandro and Anna never protested. They watched over me, they were well-behaved. They tried, in their way, not only to not be a burden but also to make me look good in front of my students and colleagues. Nevertheless, after a short while, I gave up, and rushed back to hand them to Vanda.

—Already?, she said, tauntingly. That's it for your paternity?

I struggled to explain myself. In the end I muttered something about how it was hard for me to face up to the demands of our children as she'd always done. She misunderstood, believing I wanted to come back to the family. She brightened, and talked about the new equilibrium that the four of us had to find again. I shook my head. I said:

—I have to figure things out.

In a fraction of a second Vanda read in my eyes the strength I summoned from the well-being I enjoyed without her and she understood in a flash that nothing would hold me back, not even the kids. I acknowledged, for a moment, that what I was doing to her was particularly cruel. And to avoid thinking about it I ran away.

The last sign of her arrived by mail months later. It was a thin set of forms. The head clerk in the Court of Minors of Naples notified me that a measure had been put in place, according to which Sandro and Anna were entrusted to their mother. I could have hopped on a train, run to the head clerk, protested, shouted: I'm their father, I don't give a damn about article 133 or whatever, I'm here, it's not true that I abandoned my children, I want to stay with them. I didn't do anything.

I went on with Lidia, I went on with my work.

6.

Seated, devastated, on the floor of my study, I examined that document for a long time. It was there in the yellow envelope along with Vanda's letters. I asked myself if my children had ever read the original measure decreed, as they say, by the judicial authority, or some similar document that must be somewhere, too. That sheet of paper constitutes the record of my formal renunciation of them. It's proof on paper that I abandoned them to grow up without me, that I let them fall definitively out of my life, in a tempest that would sweep them far from my eyes and from my concerns. That laconic notice proved that I'd freed myself from all that. I would get used to not feeling the weight in my head and heart and stomach anymore, because there would no longer be a daily habit, because they would soon become different from what I knew. They would lose their childish features, they would grow taller, their entire bodies would change: their faces, voices, steps, thoughts. Memory, on the other hand, would have arrested them in the final moment I'd taken them back to their mother and said: I have to figure things out.

Some time passed. I endured the separation thanks to Lidia's presence and increasingly fulfilling commitments. I left the frustrating university job. I started writing for newspapers, I launched radio shows, I turned up timidly on television. There is a distance that cannot be measured in kilometers or even in light years; it's the distance born from change. I distanced myself from my wife and my children by pursuing what excited me: the new woman I loved and engaging work, also new, which, in a sequence of apparently unstoppable events, led to one small personal success after another. Lidia liked me, everyone liked me. And meanwhile a thin fog concealed a past in which I felt slow and inconclusive. The house in Naples faded. Relatives faded, and friends. Vanda, Sandro and Anna remained alive, persistent, but only until distance drained energy from them, diminishing the pain. To this, almost automatically, I added an old mental habit. Ever since I was young I had trained myself to ignore my mother's suffering when my father tormented her. I'd become so good at it that, although I was there, I could block out the screams, the insults, the sound of him slapping her, the tears, certain sentences in dialect repeated as if they were a litany: I'll kill myself, I'll throw myself out the window. I learned not to hear my parents. As for not seeing them, all I had to do was close my eyes. I resorted to this childish trick all my life, in thousands of situations. In those days it was extremely useful, and I relied on it heavily. I had left a void, I was creating a void. My wife, my children, emerged in a wide range of moments, and nevertheless I didn't see them or hear them.

But I didn't always manage so well. I was abroad when I received news that my wife had tried to kill herself. To go that far, I cried out, desolate, but even now I don't know what I wanted to say. Maybe *that far* was a silent scream against Vanda. I asked what it meant to push oneself to the brink of death. Or more likely I was angry with myself: You've pushed her this far, shame on you. Or more generally I protested against the diffuse yearning to expect all that we desired, not caring about the risk for others, the damage we'd done. I racked my brains, distraught. Vanda was in the hospital. When and how had it happened? How would her act mark Sandro and Anna? The moments realigned, shedding new clarity on those distant figures. I realized that I was forced to choose: either leave everything, work, my life, the pattern I was creating for myself together with Lidia, and rush to cancel the void, and put everything back in order; or limit myself to calling, asking how Vanda was doing, but not seeing her, not alone, not with the children standing by her, not exposing myself to the tidal wave of emotion, not running that risk. For a long time I wavered between those two possibilities. It seemed to me that I couldn't ask anyone for advice; the responsibility of choosing was up to me. What if my wife hadn't survived? Would I have to admit to having killed her? How? By devastating her, leading her to decide that, instead of clinging to life, to the children, it was better to throw it all away? Would Sandro and Anna, growing up, turn me into the assassin? On the other hand, did she need to die so that I could realize that I'd committed a protracted crime, one lasting months and years? Crime, crime, crime.

I had demolished a life: I had pushed a young person, who, like me, wanted wholeheartedly to make something of herself, to admit that she didn't know how to live anymore.

No, what was entering my mind? Was pursuing one's destiny a crime? Was refusing to undermine one's potential a crime? Was fighting against institutions and suffocating habits a crime? How absurd.

I loved Vanda, there hadn't been a single moment in which I coldly wanted to cause her harm. I had behaved cautiously, lying precisely so that she would suffer as little as possible. But, God help me, not to the point of my own suffering, suffocating myself to keep her from suffocating. *Not that far.*

I didn't go to see her. I didn't want to know how she was. I didn't write to her. I didn't concern myself with how the children had taken it. I decided to behave so as to make it clear, for one and for all, how things stood: Nothing, not even her death, could prevent me from loving Lidia. To love: I began to utter the verb in that very period—before it had seemed to me the stuff of romance novels—convinced that I was giving it a meaning it had never had before.

7.

Vanda restabilized, she stopped seeking me out, she soon stopped writing to me. But in March of 1978 I was the one to send her a letter, asking if I could see Sandro and Anna alone.

It's hard to say why I did it. On the surface everything was sailing along. I was living in Rome. I had started working regularly for TV. I was very happy with Lidia. My wife no longer put pressure on me. The kids were simply a jolt. I would turn around suddenly when I heard a young voice on the street call out *dad*. And yet something was off-kilter. Maybe those weren't good times. My insecurities were creeping back, now and then I thought I didn't have the talent I'd imagined. There were dark moments when I convinced myself that my growing success was the result of something random, that the trend would reverse, that I would be punished for arrogantly assuming responsibilities I wasn't qualified for. But maybe Lidia also had something to do with it. I loved her even more, attributing to her a refinement, an intelligence, a sensitivity that I was increasingly less sure of deserving.

—Why are you with me? I would ask.

—Because it happened.

—That doesn't mean anything.

—But that's how it is.

—And if everything ends?

—Let's try to prevent that.

I would observe her, sometimes, from afar, at a party or some public occasion. In a few years she had stopped being a young girl. She was now a woman, quite respected, and she emanated a sinuous, fiery strength that blazed with discretion. She'll leave me soon, I would think, looking at her. Meeting her had triggered an outpouring of vitality that overwhelmed me, causing me to take the ambitious leap that rendered me a successful man. One of these days she'd realize that she'd fallen in love not with me but with the effects of her own warmth, and she would understand that, really, I was just a small, anxious man. The more she saw me for what I was, the more forcefully she'd feel attracted to others. This was what I was thinking, and recently I'd started to keep an eye on her friendships. I grew alarmed if she excessively praised this one or that. But I also feared that I was turning myself, almost without realizing it, from unbridled lover to jail-keeper. A metamorphosis—I knew well—that was totally useless. Whether I wanted it or not, Lidia would have pursued her desire, ruining me, just as I had ruined Vanda in pursuing mine. She would have betrayed me, yes, it was the right verb, even though we hadn't signed agreements, even though our relationship was free of bonds, even though I didn't feel obligated to not desire other women and she hadn't promised to not desire other men. The mere idea that it might happen destroyed me. She'll go away for work and she'll meet someone she'll like. She'll be attracted to friends or acquaintances and she'll hook up with them. She'll go to a party, she'll be in high spirits, she'll let herself go. She'll feel valued by men with authority, and in their shadow she'll enjoy privileges that I don't know how to provide. The new era has only spread out a flashy veil over the old one, archaic impulses fester under the rouge of modernity. But this is life these days and she'll live it fully, my suffering won't be able to hinder her. Which was why, sometimes, I didn't feel like working. My capacity for invention was dimming, and it wouldn't reignite unless I found a way to convince myself that I was wrong, that she loved me and always would. Otherwise what was the point of the trail of pain I'd left behind?

In those moments the tight mesh of the days—meetings, rivalries, permanent tensions, small defeats, small victories, trips for work, kisses and embraces in the evening, at night, in the morning: a perfect antidote for keeping memory and remorse at bay—slackened imperceptibly. Fathers who played with their children, those who gave erudite explanations on trains or buses, those who risked heart attacks in order to teach them how to ride a bike, grasping the seat and yelling, *pedal, pedal,* were paving the way. Vanda and the children—forgotten—reappeared, reminding me that in the past I would have done the same things. One cold morning when I was feeling particularly depressed I saw a skinny, slovenly woman on Via

Nazionale dragging two wretched children behind her, a boy and girl who were fighting amongst themselves, one around ten years old, the other around five. I looked at them for a long time. The children were pushing and insulting each other, the mother was threatening them. She had a cheap unfashionable coat, and they wore beat-up shoes. I thought, that's my family, returned from oblivion. I saw my empty place beside them; that void, I convinced myself, had turned them into this.

A few days later I wrote to Vanda. She replied after two weeks, when the three of them had receded once more to the background of my days and I was feeling decent again, having driven those nasty thoughts away. The letter got on my nerves. *You write that you need to reestablish a relationship with the children. You believe, now that four years have gone by, that it's possible to face the problem calmly. But what is there left to face? Wasn't the nature of your need precisely defined when you skipped out, robbing us of our life? When you abandoned them because you couldn't handle the responsibility? In any case I read them your request and they've decided to meet you. I remind you, in case you've forgotten, that Sandro is thirteen, and Anna nine. They're crushed by uncertainty and fear. Don't make it worse for them.* I went unwillingly to meet my children.

8.

Vanda's sarcastic reminder—*Sandro is thirteen, and Anna nine*—had prepared me to find them different from how I remembered them. But they weren't simply different: They seemed strangers who looked at me as if I were a stranger.

I took them to a café, I filled the table with good things to eat and drink. I tried to converse with them, but I ended up talking about myself. They never called me Dad. I on the other hand, anxious, said their names a thousand times. Since I feared that they remembered me only for the earthquake I'd caused in their lives, for how I'd made them suffer, I tried in a muddled way to present myself as a respectable person, mild-mannered, with a job that they could brag about to their class-mates. It seemed to me, from their attentive gazes, from an occasional smile, even from Anna's cheerful laughter, that I'd convinced them. I hoped that they would want to know, for example, what they would have to do in order to follow in my footsteps as adults. But Sandro didn't say anything, and Anna asked, nodding to her brother:

—Is it true that it was you who taught him how to tie his shoes?

I felt embarrassed. Had I taught Sandro to tie his shoes? I didn't remember. And at that point, for no precise reason, I no longer marveled that they were strangers to me; the sense of estrangement was intrinsic to our original bond. All the time I had lived with them I'd been a distracted father who didn't feel the need to know them in order to recognize them. Now, in order to make a good impression, wanting to absorb every-thing about them, I observed my children with excessive atten-tion—that, precisely, of strangers—devouring details, yearning to know them fully in a few minutes. I replied, lying: Yes, I think so, I taught Sandro lots of things, maybe also how to tie his shoes. And Sandro muttered: no one ties their shoes the way I do. Meanwhile Anna told me: It's ridiculous how he ties them, I don't believe you tie them like that, too.

I forced myself to smile, assuming the most benevolent expression I could muster. I took it for granted that I tied my shoes like anyone else: The anomaly that my two children insisted upon, each in their own way, was something that Sandro must have picked up as a child, from who knows what source. He's convinced, I thought, worried, that he's main-tained a true bond with me because of the way he ties his shoes, and now he risks discovering that he was wrong. What was I supposed to do?

Anna looked me straight in the eyes. She had a face that was always amused, a spontaneous grin that made her look happy even when she wasn't. She said: Show us how you do it, and I realized that she, too, while teasing her brother with that business about the laces, was searching for proof that I wasn't some random man they needed to think of as a father, but something more. I asked: Do you want me to show you now, here, how I tie my shoes? Yes, Anna said. I unlaced a shoe, then I laced it again. I pulled the two ends of the string, I crossed them, I passed one end under the other, I pulled tight. I looked at them. They both had their eyes trained on my shoe, their mouths half-open. Somewhat nervous, I went back to crossing the ends, again I passed one under the other, I pulled once more, I made a loop. I paused, uncertain. Sandro's eyes started to light up with satisfaction. Anna said softly: And then? I grasped the loop, I closed by pulling it between my fingers, I passed it under the end that remained, I formed another hole and pulled. There, I said to Sandro, is that how you do it? Yes, he replied. And Anna said, it's true, only the two of you tie your shoes like that, I want to learn, too.

Sandro and I spent the rest of the time tying and untying our laces until Anna, kneeling in front of the two of us, learned properly how to tie them as we did. Now and then she said: But it's ridiculous to tie them this way. In the end Sandro asked me: When did you teach me? I decided to be honest: I don't think I taught you. You learned on your own, watching me. And from that moment I started to feel guilty like never before.

Vanda wrote to me later, using hostile words to say that the two children had found me fleeting, as usual, that I had disappointed them. No mention of the laces, Sandro and Anna almost certainly hadn't told her about it. But I knew that that tying and untying had brought us closer together, or maybe it had brought us to a gap that, since their birth, had never been so slight. At least I hoped so, I wanted to believe that that was what happened. At the café I'd understood my children much more than in the past, and I had felt—felt in every pore of my body—the responsibility of what I'd wrested from them, the damage I had caused by robbing them of steadfast affection, and I cried for days and nights, making sure Lidia wasn't aware of it. Which was why I couldn't believe that they'd said to their mother: He disappointed us. But since I was sure that Vanda wasn't lying—she never lied—I thought that it was Sandro and Anna who had lied. They'd done so with good reason. They feared that if they told their mother that it had been good to see me, it would have made her suffer, and by now every time she suffered it terrified them. They preferred to say nothing about how they'd found me kind, so that Vanda wasn't upset by it.

It was during that time that I remembered when my mother had cut her wrist with my father's razor. The blood dripped onto the floor, and we children were quick to prevent her from cutting the other one as well. Something, on the shield of insensitivity that I had constructed during childhood and early adolescence in front of scenes like that, gave way. The distant torments of my mother her malcontent, the anger, at times the hatred toward the husband she'd been dealt—assaulted me without a filter, with a force I had never perceived. The pain of Vanda also passed through that breach. And for the first time I felt in my bones how much I had demolished her. And I realized with the same unbearable intensity that, while I had been keen to avoid the blows of that suffering, our two children had been struck, perhaps bludgeoned. Nevertheless they asked about the laces. Do you tie your shoes like I do? You're ridiculous, but can you teach me?

9.

I went back to see them. I turned up in their house in Naples trying to give continuity to my visits. I invited them to Rome. I took them to lunch, to dinner, to restaurants—a new experience for them—and to sleep in the apartment that I'd rented in Viale Mazzini, where I'd been living with Lidia for a short while. I realized that even if my recent successes were to have multiplied, they would never be able to justify the trail of pain that I had left behind, and I complicated my life to the point of neglecting my work. But by now that pain dwelled in gestures, in voices, indelible. Anna immediately spurned Lidia's congeniality and routinely made it clear that she couldn't stand her. Sandro, after a few sulky attempts to accept the situation, refused to set foot in a house where I lived with a woman other than his mother. They demanded my full attention, they wanted me to be available at every moment. Working little or not at all started to get me in trouble, and to deal with it I was forced to take away time from Lidia. My life with her, the free life we'd lived, lost ground. I had to take stock of contractual deadlines, Vanda's shadow, Sandro and Anna's tantrums.

—Take care of your children, Lidia told me one day.

—And you?

—I can wait.

—No, you won't wait for me. You have your work, your friends, you'll leave me.

—I said I'll wait for you.

But she wasn't happy. She had an increasingly autonomous life, without me. And the two kids weren't happy, nor did Vanda seem happy. No matter how much I dedicated myself to the children, respecting minutely all the obligations that were imposed on me, she kept stepping up her demands. I decided, for example, to see Sandro and Anna only in the house in Naples, in part because it was there that they went to school and had friends, in part because I didn't mean to further complicate Lidia's life, in part because this was what Vanda wanted. She wavered between rancor and a warm welcome. If for some reason I vexed her, she cut me off, rudely. But if I appeared docile she hosted me politely in the house, letting me work, telling the kids not to bother me, and at a certain point she started setting a place for me at lunch and at dinner as well.

It was soon the case that meeting Sandro and Anna at Vanda's home became more convenient—and also more productive in terms of work—than seeing them in Rome. Once when Lidia went away for her job—she had to be away for a week—I yielded to the insistence of both kids and went to Naples. I stayed, not for a night but for all seven days. One evening Vanda and I talked for a long time about when we'd met, almost twenty years earlier. We lay back on our old double bed without touching one another, and we fell asleep talking about those distant times. When I saw Lidia again I told her about it. In that phase I was irritated by her work obligations, by the consent that must have been growing in her, the tolerance with which she accepted the complicated situation I'd thrust her into. She was always kind, and she never got upset when the kids and my wife—we had never legally separated, and as a result that novelty, divorce, wasn't even possible—intruded with endless phone calls on our private life. Lidia didn't put forth demands, she didn't protest, she grew tense only if I had a problem with her ongoing commitments, and this made me suspect that she no longer cared about me, about us. I hoped that she would get angry, scream, cry. Instead she said nothing, she just turned pale. Then, without arguing, she left the house we'd rented together and went back to the study she'd lived in before. To my protests, my pleading, she simply replied: I need my space the way you need yours.

For a while I lived alone, in sadness. I returned to Naples, to my children, to my wife, first for a week, then two, then three. But I couldn't cope without Lidia. For several months I called her obsessively, making sure neither the kids nor Vanda were aware of it. Lidia answered right away, she talked to me affectionately, but when I told her I needed, urgently, to see her she hung up without even saying goodbye. She cut off all ties only when, ground down by the need for her and by the growing solidity of the relationship with Vanda and the kids, I proposed a sort of clandestine affair, without commitment, in which she and I were both free, based simply on the pleasure of being together once in a while. It was a terrible time. To numb the pain I dedicated all my energy to a TV show that enjoyed considerable success, and I began to earn so much money that I moved my family to the capital.

10.

I can't say precisely when I started to be afraid of Vanda. Then again, I never said to myself in such an explicit way—*I am afraid of Vanda*—it's the first time I'm trying to lend this feeling a grammar and syntax. But it's hard. Even the verb I've used—to fear—seems inadequate to me. I'm using it out of convenience, but it's limited, it leaves out a lot. In any case, for simplicity's sake, this is how things are: Since 1980 until today I've lived with a woman who, though of minute build, quite thin, fragile by now in her very bones, knows how to sap me of my voice and my strength, knows how to render me ignoble.

It happened, I think, little by little. She accepted me again, but not with the mellow love that had characterized the first twelve years of our marriage. She did so in a strenuous way, and with a thirst for self-celebration. She talked a lot about the work she'd done on herself, how she'd swept away all the taboos, her determination to fully become a woman. And so began a long period in which, it seemed to me, she wasn't able to gain equilibrium. She was worn out, her eyes and her hands never stopped moving, she was smoking a lot. She didn't want the two of us to pick up from before the crisis exploded, she refused to resemble herself. And she imposed on me a sort of daily performance aimed to show how young she was, how beautiful, how free, so much more than the young girl for whom I'd left her.

I was baffled. Almost certainly I tried to make her understand that her previous, placid attention toward me was enough, that there was no need to put so much effort into everything. But at every sign of my unhappiness, I realized, she stiffened. I'd thought that, proud of her victory, she would forget, and in fact she really was forgetting, but not as I'd imagined. She avoided throwing what I'd done in my face, she let the humiliations and insults fade. But the pain of those years, refusing to subside, only sought other outlets. Vanda continued to suffer, imbuing her suffering with a form of intolerance. She suffered and turned irritable, she suffered and turned hostile. She suffered and assumed an insulting tone, she suffered and grew inflexible. Every day of our new life was, for her, a crucial test which boiled down to: I'm no longer the accommodating person I used to be, and if you don't do what I say, get out.

I discovered that her illness depressed me. If the pain that I had inflicted on her had struggled to reach me, I was immediately attuned to the new slant of her torment and I felt the weight of it, the compunction. Slowly, filled with a sense of guilt, I put my discomfort at bay, forcing myself to pay her several compliments daily, waiting patiently for her to tire of displaying her intelligence, the radical nature of her political opinions, her recklessness in bed, her self-confidence. This yielded good results. She stopped hurling quotations in my

face, she let go of the desire to be subversive, her sex drive settled down, she went back to taking sensible care of herself.
And yet, she didn't cease to brood over every small divergence
on my part. If I happened to disagree with her, she grew
alarmed. She couldn't bear any unhappiness: She would turn
pale, light a cigarette and drag on it in brief spurts with trembling hands. She defended her positions, pressing them to
ridiculous lengths. She calmed down only if I said, in the end,
that she was right. At that moment her mood abruptly
changed, and she became excessively cheerful and obliging. I
soon understood that if, in the past, it was she who always
agreed with me, and that our closeness calmed her, now she
calmed down only if that closeness was based on the fact that
I agreed with her. Every time I contradicted her it must have
seemed a sign of some crisis, and her very alarm exasperated
her, she was the one prepared to call it quits. I learned not to
interfere in her business, to stay silent about my own, to always
appear cheerfully agreeable.

This happened, more or less, in the two years following our
reconciliation. It was a complicated two years. Then Vanda
found a balance. Wanting a job of her own, even though I
made good money, she started working in an accounting firm.
Though ever more haggard, ever thinner, she multiplied her
energy, never neglecting the house, me, or the children. I was
mindful to watch my step. I supported her distractedly in her
disputes at work, I was the mute spectator of her harassment
of cleaning ladies, I respected the iron-clad law of our domestic life. I asked her to accompany me to every public event, and
she willingly agreed. She observed everything and everyone,
and when we came home she dismantled piece by piece the
vanity of famous men, the traits of the women who had been a
little too friendly with me—the sugary voices, the fake beauty,
the pretentious chatter—ably ridiculing one and all to enter-
tain me.

The only place I tried to put in my two cents was the children's education. It rankled me that she imposed such an ascetic life on the kids: no superfluous spending, hardly any television, little music, rare outings at night, a great deal of studying. When Sandro and Anna, now for one reason, now for another, asked me wordlessly to use my authority to their advantage, I felt burdened by their glances. And since I believed I'd returned home because I loved them, in the beginning I said to myself: Be a father, you need to intervene here, you can do no less. And in fact I intervened, especially when they'd commit some infraction and she'd require them to discuss it at length, calmly, though imprisoning them inside her relentless logic. I wasn't able to hold back; in those instances, though carefully, cautiously mediating, I said my piece. Vanda was silent, she let me talk, the kids perked up, Anna threw me looks of gratitude. But then? Then a few seconds passed and their mother behaved as if she hadn't heard me, or as if I'd uttered nonsense that wasn't worth refuting, or even as if I didn't exist. She'd go on pressing them with even more overwrought arguments, asking: Express your opinion openly, do you agree or not?

One time, however, she flared up, she said to me coldly:

—Am I talking or are you?

—You.

—Then get out, please, and let me reason with my children.

I obeyed, disappointing the kids. Hours of hostility followed and, last but not least, at night, an all-out fight.

—I'm no good as a mother?

—That's not what I'm saying.

—You want them to grow up like Lidia?

—What does Lidia have to do with it now?

—Isn't she your ideal person?

—Stop it.

—If you want them to grow up like Lidia then you can get out, all three of you, I can't take it anymore.

I restrained myself. I didn't want her to shout, cry, fall apart again. The pain was always there, it never subsided. I started to invent distractions whenever she tormented the children with infinite questions, demanding responses as logical as they were sincere. Sandro and Anna looked at me, by now dismayed. At the start they must have asked themselves: Who is this man? What does he think? Is he going to make up his mind whether or not to come to our aid yelling: Enough, leave them in peace? Now they no longer asked themselves this. Maybe they'd also realized that that was the equilibrium. An equilibrium I could have shattered only if, to the words that Vanda always had on the tip of her tongue (*either you show me every minute that you've accepted me unconditionally or there's the door, get out*) I were ready to reply: Rant and rave as much as you want, kill yourself and your children. I can't stand you anymore, I'm leaving. But I was never able to do it. I'd already done it once, in vain.

So the years skipped along, methodically, and we became a comfortable, well-respected family. I earned a nice bit of money. With her ferocious eternal penny-pinching Vanda set aside enough of it and we bought this house steps from the Tiber. Sandro graduated from college, Anna too. They struggle to find work, they always lose it. They turn to us for money, their lives are a mess. Sandro has a child with every woman he loves. He has four of them, he sacrifices everything for the children, he thinks they're all that counts. Anna has refused to bring children into the world, believing it's one of the many uncivilized behaviors of the human race, primitive spoils. Neither of them submit their requests, at times absurd, to me; they know it's their mother who holds the reins to everything. They have seen me roaming through the house like a harmless spirit, practically mute. And they aren't wrong. My life was totally fulfilled without them. In the family I became a shadow man, silent even when Vanda celebrated with great joy *my* birthdays, when she invited *my* friends, *my* relatives. There were no more conflicts. In every situation, public or private, I either said nothing or nodded yes, absently amused; and she spoke to me with an ironic tone that was darkly allusive, superficially fond.

Irony, yes, sarcasm at times. And always on the brink between caresses and lashings. If by chance I utter the wrong sentence or cast a look without thinking, here are the harsh words that mark me, and something inside me runs to hide. As for my qualities, my merits, let's just say: Vanda has often led me, the children, the cleaning women, friends, guests, to believe that I am a good man, a good companion, that I was quite promising when I was young. But she has never been openly excited about my work, my successes, and if now and then she's tepidly appreciated them she's done it only to emphasize that they have allowed us to live well.

One time, maybe fifteen years ago—it was summer, we were on vacation—we were walking along the seashore, and she addressed me, unexpectedly, not with the usual tone but serious:

—I don't remember anything about us anymore.

I summoned the courage. I asked:

—About us when?

—Always: from the moment we met until today, until I'll die.

I avoided challenging her, nor did I joke about the meaninglessness of that temporal arc. Something glittering in the water saved me, it was a hundred-lire coin. I gathered it, I gave it to her to please her. She examined it closely, then she tossed it back into the sea.

11.

I have thought back often to those few words. At times they mean nothing to me, at times everything. Both she and I know the art of reticence. From the crisis of many years ago we have both learned that we need to hide a great deal from each other, and tell each other even less. It's worked. What Vanda says or does is almost always a signal for what she hides. And my continual agreement conceals the fact that for decades there's been nothing, absolutely nothing, that we share feelings about. In 1975, during one of our cruelly honest clashes, she yelled: This is why you had your wedding band sawed off, you want to get rid of me. And since I, almost without realizing, nodded yes— my physical being was by now out of control—Vanda slipped the ring off her finger and threw it away. The tiny circle of gold bounced against a wall, skidded off the stove, fell onto the floor racing, as if alive, under a piece of furniture. Five years later, when my return seemed final to her, the wedding band reappeared on her finger. It meant: I feel tied to you again, what about you? The mute question had the new imperative tone, it demanded an immediate reply, silent or blaring. I resisted for a few days, but I saw that she was turning the ring around her finger in an increasingly anxious way. The offer of fidelity served above all to verify my intentions. I went to a jeweler and I came back home with a gold ring around my finger; I'd had engraved, inside, the date of our reconciliation. Neither of us said anything. But in spite of the ring I had a lover almost immediately—three months after I came back home—and I've been stubbornly unfaithful up until a few years ago.

I'm not sure of the reasons why I behaved this way. Certainly the sport of seduction, sexual curiosity, and the impression (unfounded) that each flirtation reawakened lost creativity all played a role. But I prefer a motivation that's more elusive, and also more true: I wanted to prove to myself that in spite of having reformed the old couple, in spite of having returned to the family, in spite of putting a wedding band back on my finger, I was free, that I no longer had real ties.

I always put myself to the test, however, with great prudence. There wasn't a willing woman to whom I didn't say at the opportune moment, I want you, yes, but if we want to have a long friendship we have to make a clear pact; I'm a married man, I've already made my wife and children suffer beyond the pale, I don't want them to suffer again; therefore all we can indulge in is a little fun, for a brief period and with utmost discretion; if this feels right to you then let's go ahead, and if not, then no. No one ever told me to get lost. Times had changed: They increasingly obliged single women, and married ones, to relish their pleasures with confidence, as men did. Girls felt old-fashioned if they complained too much, and women with husbands and children considered adultery a venial sin or, more simply, a masculine trick to subdue them. They unleashed their desires, as a result, without expecting love of any kind, and therefore they listened to me, amused, as if my premise were an exciting little tale. Here we are, then, having a fling. In the rarest of circumstances I thought I'd lost my head, and I feared that it was about to start all over again. It happened mainly when it was my lover who said, enough. In those cases the wound left by Lidia opened up again, and for a few weeks, a few months, I felt like I would die.

But it didn't happen, and it was the very ghost of Lidia that saved me from further devastation. I didn't waste my time over any other woman because I was still tied to her. I never forgot Lidia, thinking of her still upsets me. Which is why there has never been a year in which I haven't figured out a way to meet her. I've assiduously followed developments in her life. She still teaches at the university, but she's close to retiring. She writes for newspapers, she's an admired economist, all the more so in these times of unemployment and hardship. She got married thirty years ago to a fairly well-known writer, the kind who enjoys a certain renown all his life and then, as soon as he dies, is never read again. It's a successful marriage. She has three sons, all of them grown men by now, who all work abroad in well-paid, prominent positions. I'm happy for her, it's wonderful that she's had a happy life. At first she didn't want to see me. I'd wait for her under the foyer to her building, spying her from afar, seduced by her clothes, their carefully-combined colors, her elegant gait; but over the years she's yielded. Meeting up has become one of our habits, almost a yearly ritual which continues to thrill me. They were and remain innocent meetings. When we see each other, she talks a lot about herself. I listen to her, attentive. Her life has become progressively fuller than mine, and now that satisfactions tend to diminish for her as well, she goes on at length, tenderly, about the successes of her sons. The husband knows all about us. I think she even tells him about my complaints as a crotchety old man, and the troubles that Sandro and Anna gave me, and give me still. Vanda, meanwhile, has no idea that I have never lost contact with the woman for whom, once, long ago, I left her. I don't want to think about what would happen were she to know about it; Lidia's name alone has been unutterable for four decades. I'm sure she could withstand the entire list of my lovers, but not the proof that I see Lidia, that I'm in touch with her, that I love her still.

CHAPTER THREE

1.

I woke up with a start. I was still in the study, but lying on one side on top of Vanda's letters. The electric light had stayed on, but through the shutters, through rosy slits, the day now arrived. I had slept amid the fury, supplications and tears of forty years ago.

I pulled myself up. My back hurt, so did my neck and my right hand. I tried to stand up but I couldn't. I had to get on all fours in order to lift myself up with a groan, clutching the bookcase. I felt a stab of anguish in my chest, it came from a dream that still dazed me. What had I dreamed? I was there, in the upside-down study. Lidia was stretched out on the floor amongst all the books, appearing as she had years ago. Looking at her, I felt even older, and I didn't feel joy but discomfort. My whole house was departing from Rome. It moved slowly, barely wavering, like a boat on a canal. For a while that motion seemed completely normal to me, then I realized something was wrong. The apartment in its entirety was heading toward Venice, and nevertheless, beyond any logic, it was leaving a part of itself behind. I couldn't understand how there were two studies, identical in every detail, including my presence and Lidia's, but one remained immobile, isolated, and the other backed away along with the rest of the house. Then I realized, on second glance, that the girl traveling with me toward Venice wasn't Lidia but the one from the solenoid. The revelation took my breath away.

I looked at my watch. It was five twenty. My right leg also

hurt. With some effort I pulled up the shutter, opened the glass door, and stepped onto the balcony to rouse myself definitively with fresh air. Birds were singing, insistently, and I saw cold rectangles of sky among the buildings. I said to myself: I have to get rid of those letters before Vanda wakes up. She would have despised the fact that the thieves had brought them back into the open, that they were there, on the floor, that I'd read them—read them, not reread them—as if I'd only received them that night. She probably didn't even remember writing them. She would have gotten angry, and with good reason. It was unbearable that words born from an imbalance, from a vanished age and culture, had resurfaced out of the blue. Those sentences were her but not her, remnants of a voice she'd shed. I quickly returned the room. I gathered up the letters and tossed them into the trash.

At that point I wondered what to do. Make myself a coffee? Wake myself up with a shower? Make sure right away that there were no other painful documents lying around? I reexamined the room, looking hard: the floor, the furniture, the garbage bags, the dismantled shelves, the ceiling. I paused at the cube from Prague, the cube containing my secrets. It was leaning precariously, it almost looked as if it might fall, it seemed necessary to push it back. But first I strained my ears to make sure Vanda was still sleeping. Since the singing of the birds was so loud that it canceled all other sounds, I opened one door after the next, making sure the handles squeaked as little as possible, and on tiptoe I went into the bedroom. I saw my wife in the half-light: She was a small elderly woman who slept with her mouth half-open, her breath calm. It occurred to me that she was dreaming, that she was feeling something. She must have set aside the logic with which she had defended herself her whole life from me, from the children, from the world, and now she'd surrendered to herself. But I knew nothing of that inner turmoil, I would never know it. I kissed her forehead. Her breath paused for an instant, then resumed.

I closed, with equal attention, all the doors behind me, and I returned to the study. When I'd reached the top of the metal ladder, I opened the blue cube, pressing hard on one of its sides. It was empty.

2.

The cube from Prague had contained, for decades, twenty-odd Polaroids taken between 1976 and 1978. It was I who'd bought the camera. Back then I took pictures of Lidia, constantly. While the ordinary cameras meant that if you weren't able to print the rolls of film on your own, you had take them to a photographer, thereby subjecting your private life to the eyes of a stranger, with that device you shot and printed right away. Lidia came up beside me just in time to assist with the miracle, when the reproduction of her thin body was already emerging from the thick fog of a little rectangle of paper expelled by the camera. I accumulated several Polaroids in those years. When I returned to Vanda I brought back those in which, photographing Lidia, I thought I was photographing my delight in being alive. In most of the images she was nude.

I remained on top of the ladder, stunned. For some reason that I struggled to clarify to myself, I thought of Labes again, after not having thought about him all night. He'd gone to his girlfriend's place, the young carabiniere had said, laughing. Everyone laughs about sex, even though we all know that it can sow discord, make us unhappy, generate violence, drive us to desperation and death. Who knows how many friends and acquaintances had smiled or laughed, when I'd left home. They'd been amused (Aldo's out enjoying himself, hahaha) just like Nadar, the carabiniere and I, at the thought of Labes's erotic wanderings. But I'd come back, Labes no, not yet. No mewing, just the birdsong. I thought of Vanda. She'd looked at me, annoyed, not laughing at the carabiniere's remark. In her mind Labes had been sequestered, and sooner or later the thieves would be asking for a ransom. But none of the men had taken the old lady's notion seriously, the carabiniere above all: Gypsies don't steal cats to get money in exchange. Certainly—I said to myself at the top of the ladder—not gypsies. And I realized why I had suddenly remembered Labes. The photos and the cat had eros and disappearance in common. The thieves weren't Roma kids and they weren't searching for some little trinket. They ransacked homes to locate the weak points of their inhabitants, and then they got in touch, asking for money.

I thought back to how the solenoid girl was paying attention to the cat—how her vivid gaze ran back and forth across books, knickknacks, the blue cube. She'd had her eyes on this last item straightaway, even though it was up high and in an inconspicuous spot. Nice color, she'd said. What a trained eye. I felt the anger rising to my head and I tried to calm down. At my age it's easy to turn a suspicion into a valid hypothesis, a valid hypothesis into an absolute certainty, an absolute certainty into an obsession. I stepped down carefully, rung by rung. That hypothesis risked leading me astray. I had to verify, first of all, that nothing more obvious had happened, more immediately risky. The thieves—I drove away the girl with an act of sheer will, I went back to that generic noun—had found the cube. They had been able to open it, but maybe at most they'd laughed a bit and then tossed the pictures among the thousands of other things that had spilled down from the shelves and the loft. It was the most likely thing. In that case, however—I said to myself—I have to go back and check everything right away, here and in the other rooms. Vanda mustn't find the Polaroids, it would be a disgrace. What would the acquiescence of all those years have amounted to, all that discretion, our ongoing repression, if now, in the end, in old age, when we are particularly fragile, when we need to help each other, we end up butchering each other instead? I made myself reexamine every corner carefully and I began to rummage through what was piled up against the bookcase, hoping the pictures had been under my nose all night without my realizing.

But the more I rummaged, the more I grew distracted. I thought of Lidia, about our happy time together. Had I found the photos, I would have tossed them out in the trash as I'd done with the letters. And yet I couldn't bear the thought that they would disappear forever, that I couldn't, now and again, when I was alone at home, look at them, rejoice, console myself, grow melancholy, feel that at least for a brief segment of my life I'd been happy. The joy of those days, its soft breath without any poisonous aftertaste, already seemed to me, at times, a senile fantasy, the hallucination of a brain lacking oxygen. What would have happened next? I rummaged with an incongruous combination of frenzy and apathy. I convinced myself that the photos were neither in the study nor in the living room. Well then? In a little while Vanda would be up and about again, and with an efficiency surpassing mine she would have busied herself, tidying up. Her gaze didn't cloud over losing itself in daydreams, she was always alert. The Polaroids could have ended up in the bedroom, in the rooms that had once been Sandro's and Anna's. If she were to find them, not only would she discover that Lidia had never been forgotten, had endured for decades in an intangible youth, whereas she had inevitably aged before my eyes, at my fingertips. It would also be the case that, in an attempt to placate her, I would have to destroy the photos in her presence, burning them over the stove without even a last look.

I opened the door once more without a squeak. I went into Anna's room. There too, what a disaster. I started to search though hundreds of postcards, newspaper clippings, pictures of actors and singers, brightly-colored drawings, pens that no longer wrote, rulers, T squares, everything. Then I heard the bedroom door opening, Vanda's footsteps. Pale, her eyes puffy, she appeared in the doorway.

—Did you find Labes?

—No, I would have woken you up right away.

—Did you sleep?

—Only a little.

3.

We had breakfast, saying hardly a word to one another, as usual. I only tried, at a certain point, to send her back to bed, but she refused. When she locked herself in the bathroom I sighed in relief and started hurriedly to look through Sandro's old room. But there wasn't enough time, Vanda reappeared twenty minutes later with her hair still wet, her face marked by her foul mood, yet nevertheless ready to reorganize her house from top to bottom.

—What are you looking for? she asked, perplexed.

—Nothing, I'm setting things right.

—It doesn't look like it.

I felt in the way. She had never trusted me to help, she was always convinced that she could do it better and more quickly on her own. Offended, I replied:

—Did you see how I straightened up in the living room and the study?

She went to see. She looked dissatisfied.

—Are you sure you haven't thrown out things we need?
—I only got rid of what was ruined.
She shook her head, unconvinced, and I feared she wanted to start rummaging through the garbage bags.
—Trust me, I said.
She grumbled:
The bags are in the way, take them down to the dumpsters.
I panicked. I didn't want to leave her in the house alone. I hoped to keep up with her and, if the photos were somewhere, get to them before she did.
—Maybe it's better if you help me—I said—there are a lot of them.
—Make multiple trips. Someone needs to stay here.
—Why?
—They might call.
She continued to believe that the thieves would turn up and that they would give Labes back to us. Her conviction got to me. I went back to suspecting the solenoid girl. She would have been the one to call. Or maybe not, maybe her likely accomplice would have called, the man with the fake leather jackets. I said:
—They'll want to talk to me.
—I don't think so.
—Usually one talks to the man.
—That's nonsense.
—Are you really willing to pay for the cat?
—You want them to kill him?
—No.
I heard the voices of the girl and the man in my head, the chuckers, the guffaws. For the cat—they would have said—we want this price, and for the photos another. If not? If not we show the photos to your wife. Of course, I could have responded: That girl is my wife when she was young, but they would have started no doubt to laugh, they would have replied: No problem,

then, we'll return them to your wife along with the cat. Like that, all of it predictable. I tried to take my time, I sighed:

—There's so much violence these days.

—There always has been.

—But it never entered the house.

—You think so?

I didn't reply. She said, abruptly,

—Well, are you going?

I bent down to pick up a piece of glass I'd overlooked.

—Maybe it's easier to clean the whole house first, and then take down the garbage.

—I need space, go.

I put all the bags in the elevator, and in the end there was no room for me. I descended on foot to the ground floor, I pressed the elevator button, the car came down. I dragged the bags to the dumpsters. They were huge and inflated, they didn't fit in the bin for paper, nor in the one for glass or for plastic, nowhere. I would have to start sorting though the stuff piece by piece. I let it go. I abandoned the bags on the pavement, neatly arranged, however, hoping Nadar didn't see me through his window.

It was already hot, I dried off the sweat. The hypothetical gaze of Nadar made me think of other gazes. Why was I convinced that the thieves would get in touch by phone? They could already be out there somewhere, watching me. The young man of color leaning against one of the few cars, the only human being on the still, empty street, couldn't he be one of them? I went back to the door of the building, surveying the boy out of the corner of my eye. My heart was racing, my whole body felt bloated, my neck hurt. For the first time I wished that Sandro or Anna would show up suddenly, that they would give me a hand, that they would pull me, above all, out of my congealing old blood, teasing me affectionately as they usually did: You exaggerate, you see dangers and conspiracies everywhere, you don't know how to live in the real world, you keep writing those films for TV in your head that you stopped writing ten years ago.

I went back into the house, anxious; a glance would be enough to know if, in the meantime, Vanda had found the pictures. I quickly prepared a few conciliatory words to use if need be: I know nothing about them, who knows where they came from, give them to me and I'll throw them out as well. I also thought about insisting on the need for order: The house, reduced to that state, seemed an incentive to stir things up even more. Vanda also seemed to think the same thing, given that she woke up so early to start working. But when I appeared in the living room it didn't look like she'd done much. I surprised my wife, who was rummaging in a corner as if she'd lost something. The moment she heard me she stood up, setting her lips straight, smoothing her flimsy dress with her hands.

4.

The day turned sweltry. I left the living room and the study to Vanda and I went off to organize Sandro's and Anna's rooms. I assigned myself the task so that I could look calmly for the pictures. My wife never called out to me, she never made a sound, and after a while I went on to sift through the bedroom, the bathroom. When I convinced myself that the photos were nowhere and that therefore I had to anticipate the worst, I returned to the living room. I found my wife seated on the threshold of the open balcony, looking out. For all that time she'd done nothing. The room was exactly as I'd left it.

—You're not feeling well?—I asked.

—I'm perfectly fine.

—Is something wrong?

—Everything.

I said, in the kindest way I'm capable of:

—We'll get Labes back, you'll see.

She turned to look at me.

—Why did you decide to let me know, now, the reason you wanted to name him that?

—I never hid it from you. He's the beast of the house and so I called him Labes, what's wrong with that?

—You're a liar. You were always a liar, and in old age you keep telling lies.

—I don't understand you.

—You understand perfectly well: There's the Latin dictionary, on the floor.

I didn't reply. Vanda, when she wants to vent, always proceeds with tiny insignificant facts. I went into the corner that she had indicated to me with a feeble gesture. On the floor, among other books in good condition, was the Latin dictionary, open to the page where the name I'd given our cat sixteen years ago appeared. A coincidence. At first I thought that Vanda herself gave little weight to the matter. She had spoken to me without the usual irony, with a voice that was simply a means to fetter words, as if indifferent to their significance. The dictionary—she said quietly—turning to look beyond the railing of the balcony—was open to the letter L, and the word *labes* was underlined in pen, as well as its definitions, one by one. *Fall, landslide, collapse, ruin.* One of your jokes. I called the cat lovingly and you amused yourself hearing how the name, unbeknownst to me, resounded through the house in all its negativity: *disaster, misfortune, filth, infamy, shame. Shame,* you made me say. You were always like that. You act kind and meanwhile you vent your nasty feelings in deviant ways. I don't know when I realized you were like this. Early on, in any case, decades ago, maybe even before we got married. But I tied myself to you all the same. I was young, I felt attracted, I didn't know what a random thing attraction is. For years I wasn't happy, but I wasn't unhappy. I realized late that others intrigued me, neither more nor less than you did. I looked around, disoriented. At every opportunity—I said to myself—I could have a lover: It's like the rain, a drop collides randomly with another drop and forms a rivulet. All you had to do was insist on that initial curiosity, and the curiosity would become attraction, the attraction would grow and lead to sex, sex would call for repetition, repetition would establish a habit, a need. But I thought I was supposed to love only you, forever, and so I looked the other way, I kept my eyes on the children, their tantrums. How foolish. If I ever loved you—and today I'm no longer sure: Love is just a container we shove everything into—it didn't last long. You were certainly nothing special for me, nothing intense. You simply allowed me to consider myself a grown woman: Living together, sex, kids. When you left me I suffered, most of all, for that part of me I had uselessly sacrificed to you. And when I welcomed you home, I only did it to restore to myself what you'd taken. But I soon realized that, in the tangle of emotions and desires and sex and feelings, it was hard to establish what you needed to give back to me, which is why I did everything I could to send you back to Lidia. I never believed that you'd repented, that you'd realized you wanted me and no one else. I thought every day about how much you had deceived me. You felt absolutely nothing for me, not even that feeling of closeness, of sympathy, that prevents one human being from sitting by idly while another suffers to death. You'd shown me in every possible way that you loved Lidia as you'd never loved me. I knew by then that if a man loves another woman he never returns to his wife for love. And so I told myself: Let's see how long he can stand it before he runs back to her. But the more I tormented you the more you caved. *Labes*, yes, you're right. Years, decades have gone by playing this game and we've made a habit of it: living in disaster, reveling in disgrace, this was our glue. Why? Maybe for the kids. But this morning I'm not so sure about it anymore, I feel indifferent to them, too. Now that I'm nearly eighty years old I can say that I like almost nothing about my life. I don't like you, I don't like them, I don't like myself. Which is why, maybe, when you went away, I was so distraught. I felt stupid, I wasn't able to get out before you did. And I wanted with all my might for you to come back only to be able to say to you: Now I'm the one who's leaving. But look, I'm still here. As soon as you make an effort to say something clearly, you realize that it's only clear because you've simplified it.

This was the speech, more or less; I've summarized it in my own words. For the first time since we'd reconciled she strove to be explicit without growing in the least bit emotional. Now and again I interrupted her with half-sentences of tepid objection, but she didn't hear me, or she didn't want to. She forged ahead as if she were talking only to herself, and at a certain point I sealed myself off as well. I had only one question in mind: Why did she decide to talk to me in such blunt terms? Didn't she realize that many of these words can have severe consequences for our old age? I told myself: Don't get alarmed, she's not like you, she's never been afraid the way you've been ever since you were a little boy. And this is why she knows how to pile it on. Rather, growing increasingly indifferent over the years, she'll keep delighting in piling it on, she'll keep repeating this cruel conversation. So don't say anything. They've destroyed her house, she's tired, the toil she's facing depresses her. In this moment a little nudge is enough to leave everything the way it is and walk out; so, if you really need to say something, suggest calling someone who can give her a hand with this work. Convince her that it won't cost much, remind her that her bones are fragile and that she shouldn't exhaust herself; in other words, look the other way, pretend it's nothing, protect the days, the months that remain.

5.

I don't know how long my wife talked to me: a minute, two, five. What's certain is that at one point, given that I didn't react, she looked at her watch and got up.

—I'm going to buy a few things, she said. Keep an ear out for the telephone and the intercom.

I replied, solicitous:

—Go ahead, don't worry. If the thieves turn up I'll deal with it, we'll get Labes back.

She didn't reply. But when she reappeared with the shopping cart, ready to go out, she said quietly:

—The cat's gone.

I think she wanted to say that she'd lost every hope of getting him back. While she crossed the living room, the foyer, and opened the front door, she explained to me that I needed to pay attention to the phone and the buzzer not because the thieves might call, but because two weeks had gone by and the company that rented us the electric stimulator was going to send someone to pick it up that day.

—Don't let them rob you of any more money—she said, and she closed the door behind her.

But if she didn't believe in the idea of a ransom anymore, I, who knew about the disappearance of the Polaroids, realized that I believed in it even more. Not just that. I asked myself: Who will show up to pick up the stimulator, a random messenger, or that girl with the lively eyes again? I soon had no doubt that she would be the one to reappear. Time passed, my wife returned, she started cooking something. I pretended to be calm but I was extremely agitated, I got a headache. I already pictured the girl in the doorway. She would be the one to tell me: We have Labes, we have the pictures, this is the price to pay. I would ask: Or else? Or else, the girl would reply—rather she replied, replied, replied—or else we kill the cat and we deliver the pictures to the person who should have them. While eating a bit of *stracchino*, my heart, in my chest, felt enormous.

After lunch Vanda, perhaps purified after her outburst, was again her usual self. Methodically, without ever stopping, she reorganized the kitchen, the bedroom, Anna's room, Sandro's, and she also drafted a long detailed list of what needed to be fixed. She was on the phone with a carpenter she trusted, discussing the price, when I heard the intercom. I went to reply. A woman's voice told me she was there to pick up the stimulator. Was it the same girl from two weeks ago? Hard to tell, she hadn't said much. I let her in, running to a window that faced the street, and looked out. It was her. She held the door open with one hand, but she hadn't made up her mind whether or not to enter. She was talking to a man I saw from behind, partially covered by the branches of the magnolia tree. My breathing grew labored, it always happens when I get upset. From where I stood I couldn't be sure that it was the crook with the fake leather jackets, and yet my blood thickened, dulling my senses; I both hoped and dreaded that it was him. What were they talking about? What was their scheme? Would the girl have come up, the man waiting below? No, it looked as if they'd decided, they would come up together. Every story is a dead end, you always arrive at a moment like this. So what to do, go back, start again? Even though you're old enough to know that every story, sooner or later, slams up against the last word? I distinctly felt the same fear that gripped me when my father finally decided to join us at dinner. We were already sitting at the table, we'd

been there for some time. I heard his lazy footsteps in the hallway. What mood was he in, good, bad? What would he say,
what would he do? My wife—who had just stopped talking on
the phone, but who must not have heard the buzzer—yelled
at me from the bedroom:

—Can you please come here for a second? Can you help me
move the wardrobe?

BOOK THREE

CHAPTER ONE

1.

Our mother left us a few feet from the café. How old was I? Nine? Sandro had turned thirteen a few months earlier, I remember because Mom and I had made him a cake and he'd said, in front of the burning candles, that if he blew them all out in one breath he wanted a wish to come true. What is it? our mother had asked him. To meet Dad, he'd replied. And so, because of him, here we are in front of the café. I'm scared. I don't know anything about my father. I loved him once but I haven't loved him for a long time. The thought of meeting him gives me a stomachache. I don't want to tell him I have to go to the bathroom, I'm ashamed. Which is why I'm so angry at my brother, who always lays down the law, and also at my mother, who always does what he wants in the end.

2.

That's it, I don't remember anything else. But to be honest I don't care, it's just an excuse to call Sandro. I pick up the phone, his cell rings on, then the voicemail kicks in. I wait two minutes and call back. After five tries he answers meanly, saying: What do you want? I ask him without preamble: Do you remember when we met Dad in that café in Piazza Carlo III? I put on my little girl voice, affected whines and giggles, as if nothing's happened, as if I didn't try everything to take Aunt

Gianna's money from him, as if I hadn't yelled that if he really didn't want to give me even a penny he was dead to me, dead and buried, that I never wanted to see him again.

He says nothing. Meanwhile he's thinking: Forty-five years under your belt, and you're carrying on as if you were fifteen. I hear everything he's thinking. I hear the periods and the commas, and I know that he hates me. But it doesn't matter. I rattle on about Mom and Dad, about our childhood, about meeting our father years ago, about a hole in my memory that I suddenly wanted to fill. He tries to interrupt, but with me it's impossible, I don't let anyone get a word in. Without warning I say:

—Let's get together.

—I'm busy.

—Please.

—No.

—Tonight?

—You know you're busy tonight.

—Doing what?

—It's your turn to feed the cat.

—I'm not going. I haven't gone once.

—Are you kidding?

—Nope.

—You promised Mom.

—I promised, but I can't handle being in that house on my own.

We go on for a while with these sorts of sentences, arguing back and forth, until he realizes I'm serious, that our parents' week at the sea is almost over and that I've skipped all my turns. So—he says—that's why I found the house always stinking of piss, the water bowl half empty, the food dish without a scrap and Labes freaking out. He gets angry, he hisses that I'm selfish, cold, irresponsible. But I don't get upset. I follow up with fakeness, laughter, terrors true and false, self-deprecating irony. Slowly he calms down. Fine, he says with the older-brother tone he uses when he wants to flatten me. Go off to Crete with the last guy you picked up: I'll deal with Labes tonight, too, just stop being such a pain in the ass.

Silence. I change now, I always know the right moment to alter my voice, to sound pathetic, just like Mom. I say quietly: I only mentioned Crete and the new boyfriend to not worry our parents; actually, I'm not going on vacation this year, I'm broke, and I'm sick of everything.

There, I'm well aware of the kind of guy he is, now he's got his back up against the wall. He says, OK, let's go see Labes together.

3.

We meet under the doorway to our parents' building. I hate the area around Piazza Mazzini, the stink of smog and the river reaches as far as this street. Labes is mewing as if he's about to explode, we can hear it from the stairs. We go up. Gross, I say, as I enter, running to open the balconies and windows. Then I start talking to the cat. I tell him how disgusting he is, and this calms him, he runs up to rub himself against my ankles. But as soon as he hears Sandro fixing his food, he leaves me and scampers over quickly to my brother. I stay in the living room. This house makes me sad. I lived here from the age of sixteen to thirty-four. It's as if our parents, along with all their crap, had moved the worst of all the houses we've lived in into this place.

Sandro reappears, I hear Labes crunching his food in the kitchen. My brother's nervous, he's performed his little task, he wants to leave as quickly as possible. But I sit down on the couch and start up again about our childhood: our father who abandons us, our mother who flips out, our meeting with Dad. Sandro's still standing up, making clear to me that he's in a hurry. He mutters vague sentences, he feels obliged to be the affectionate child. He overflows with gratitude, he gets annoyed at me for circling around that episode in a sarcastic way.

—Bullshit, he exclaims, it was Dad who asked to meet, I have nothing to do with it. Plus it wasn't a café and it wasn't Piazza Carlo III. Mom took us to Piazza Dante and Dad was there waiting for us, under the monument.

—I remember a café and Piazza Carlo III. Dad once said it was a café.

—Either you trust me or there's no point in talking. He took us to a restaurant in Piazza Dante.

—And what happened?

—Nothing, he talked the whole time.

—What did he say?

—The gist was that he worked in television, that he met famous actors and singers, that he was right to leave Mom.

I burst out laughing.

—It's true. I think he was right, too.

—You say that now but back then you didn't sleep at night and you threw up everything you ate. You're the one who made life complicated for me and Mom, more than Dad.

—You're a liar, I never cared about him.

He shakes his head. He's swallowed the bait, he decides to have a seat.

—Do you at least remember when you told him about the laces?

Laces? My brother's like that. He likes to take a random detail and elaborate on it. Thanks to his way with small talk, women adore him. First he amuses them, and then he turns everything into melodrama. In my opinion he should have followed in Dad's footsteps instead of studying geology—worked in TV, maybe been a host, talked onscreen to ladies, young girls. I look at him, pretending to be curious about the story

he's about to tell me. He's handsome, he behaves like a gentle-
man, he satiates you with his courtesy. And he's so thin, lucky
him, with a face as slim as a teenager's. He's almost fifty but
still passes for thirty. He looks after three wives. Wives, yes,
even though he only got married once. And he has four kids,
something of a record these days: two with the first wife, the
legal one, and one with each of the others. In addition he has
girlfriends of every age that he sees regularly and to whom he
willingly lends not only a sensitive ear but a little sex if they
need it. He's a smooth operator, that's the point. He has no
money, he squandered Aunt Gianna's inheritance distributing
funds to women and offspring. He loses every job he finds and
yet he gets by without the hardships of survival that I face.
Why? Because the mothers of his kids are all well off, and even
when they move on to other men they still consider him a kind
boyfriend, a great father, so they remain a steady resource.
You'd need to see him with the kids, they love him so much.
Of course, now and again, he gets into trouble. Even for him
it's hard to maintain such a complicated web of affection, and
so vicious wars flare up, among his women, to be exclusively
his. But up until now he's managed, and I know why. My
brother is a fake. Fake even with himself. The reason he can
spread his attention and consolation so effectively among so
many women—often with moralistic advice that, coming from
his mouth, sounds truly hypocritical—is that he knows perfectly how to mime every positive feeling without ever feeling
a single one.

—What kind of laces? I ask him.

—Shoelaces. While we were eating, you asked if I'd copied
my way of tying them from him.

—Wait, how do you tie them?

—The way he ties them.

—And how does he tie them?

—A way no one else does.

—And did he know that you tied your shoes like he did?

—No, it was you who made him notice.

I honestly don't remember this. I ask:

—How did he react?

—He was moved.

—What do you mean?

—He burst into tears.

—I don't believe it. I never saw him cry.

—That's what happened.

Labes turns up cautiously. I wonder if he's come to me or to Sandro. I realize I'd like him to come to me, but only to be able to chase him away. The cat lands with a leap onto my brother's knees. I say, with a touch of spite:

—You were the one who wanted to meet him. I'm sure of it.

—Think whatever you want.

—And anyway, why did Mom agree to it? She'd stopped acting crazy by then, we were used to the fact that he wasn't around anymore. She should have said no to him. What possessed her to turn everything upside-down again?

—Forget about it.

—No, I want to know: Why?

—I was the one who insisted.

—You see how you have something to do with it?

—I insisted because you were having such a tough time.

—Oh, how generous of you.

—I was a kid. I thought that if our father saw, in person, the state you'd been reduced to, he'd realize that you needed him and come home.

—So, in your opinion, Dad backed down for me?

—Don't delude yourself.

—Well then?

—Is it possible that you don't remember anything?

—No.

—Okay, I'll tell you something else. The morning we met it was our mother who said to you: Have you noticed the ridiculous way your brother ties his shoes? Your father's fault, he's never done it right: Tell him when you see him.

—And?

—This story about the laces involves all of us. Dad came back for Mom, for me, for you. And the three of us wanted him to come back. Get it?

4.

That's Sandro for you, he knows how to sugarcoat everything in a way that's reassuring. Look at him now, the way he strokes Labes. He caresses him, he fondles him, the cat's delighted. He does this with everyone, animals and human beings. He's Mom's little darling, and Dad talks only to him about serious matters. This is how he nabs everything—affection, respect, money—and leaves only the crumbs to me. What a poser. And his version of the story about the laces is false, false, false. *He* had pressed our mother to take us to our father because *I* wasn't doing well? And the two of us moved our parent to the point of making him run back home? And our mother worked it on her end? And thus our loving family came back together? Who does he take me for, one of his admirers? I tell him:

—The only ties that counted for our parents were the ones they've tortured each other with their whole lives.

Then I get up. I take Labes off his knees, I carry him over to the balcony, caressing him. The cat squirms away at first, then yields. From there, from the balcony, I say to Sandro: Our parents have given us four very enlightening scenarios: first: Mom and Dad, happy and young, two kids frolicking in the Garden of Eden; second: Dad finds another woman and disappears with her, Mom loses it, the kids lose Eden; third: Dad has second thoughts and comes back home, the children try to get back to earthly paradise, Mom and Dad show us daily that it's a useless effort; fourth: The kids discover that there never was an Eden and that they have to make do with Hell.

My brother scowls:

—You're worse than our mother.

—You don't like Mom anymore?

—It's *you* I don't like. She's passed her defects onto you and you've warped them even more.

—Which?

—All of them.

—Give me an example.

—The listing: first, second, third, fourth. Both of you like to build enclosures and confine other people inside them.

I tell him coldly that I was limiting myself to describing the situation we had lived through together. But you have to humiliate me right away, I complain. And without reason: If I'm worse than Mom, then you're worse than Dad. You never think you have to listen; in fact, you've inherited the worst of both of them, because not only do you not listen, but just like Mom you grab onto a tiny detail and you build a mountain of bullshit on top.

He stares at me, his lips tight, shaking his head, then he looks at his watch. On the one hand he's afraid he's gone too far. On the other, he's thinking that with me there's no hope, peace isn't possible, all I can do is argue. I returned to the living room, and before he can get up to go I sit back down on the couch. Labes returns, wanting to be scratched, and to calm him I kiss him on the head. It's time to tell my brother the real reason I called him. I utter sentences like: After all, what can we do, there's no escape from chromosomes, it's neither my fault nor yours, we inherit everything, even the way we scratch our heads. And I laugh, as if I'd said something funny. Still laughing, without any preamble, I announce that I've been turning an idea around in my head for a while. I say, let's ask Mom and Dad to sell this house: It's worth at least a million and a half. We split it exactly, we can make seven hundred and fifty thousand each.

5.

Sandro looks at me, suddenly interested. There's only one thing we never argue about. It's from our mother that we get our obsession with money. Dad earned a fair amount, but he was so consumed by ambition that he barely noticed. For him work was what counted, the need for approval, the fear of losing it. Mom was always the one who took care of the money. She saved it, she hoarded it. She was the one who wanted this house. She made us feel the weight of every penny. Her love for her children morphed into money. She never hoarded it for herself, even less for Dad, but to allow the two of us to live well in the present, and safely into the future. The post-office ledger, the bank account, this apartment, were her ways to tell us she loved us. This is what I thought for a long time, maybe Sandro too. The proof that I love you—our mother showed us every day—is that I don't spend money on myself, but hoard it for you. The result, for me, is that not having money is further proof of my inability to be loved. That's why I think I was so upset with Aunt Gianna when she left almost her entire wad to Sandro. At least this is what the doctors told me when that situation drove me to a nervous breakdown and they stuffed me with pills. But it's so hard to organize my head, there's always something that doesn't make sense. This no-money no-love equation is probably correct, but then why, as soon as I have money, do I squander it? Why, as soon as someone likes me, do I drive him away? For that matter, isn't it the same for Sandro?

All those women with money, all those spoiled children, aren't they the sign of a hole that's never filled? While for our mother enjoyment—maybe the only thing she enjoyed—meant putting money aside, we feel like we're doing well only when we're spending it. We're identical, my brother and I. And in these times, when there's no money. And we're only getting older. I'm fat, I'm getting more wrinkles and gray hairs. I hate Sandro for staying as handsome as a boy: long eyelashes, green eyes, a head full of hair at fifty, still dark, no dye job, athletic build. He doesn't even exercise. He's finally listening to me. I ramble, giving him time to process my idea. I say: They're both part of a generation that was lucky, they went from poverty to a comfortable life, Dad even nabbed a little recognition, they both have a good pension, what the fuck else do they want? See what I'm saying?

At this point my brother blinks as if to erase the picture I'm painting for him and asks:

—Why do they have to sell and give us the money?

—It's our house.

—It's their house.

—Sure, but we're going to inherit it.

—So?

—So we ask them to give us an advance on our inheritance.

—And where do they go live?

—We find them a smaller apartment, two rooms and a kitchen somewhere outside the Center, and we pay the rent.

—You're crazy.

—Why? Remember Marisa?

—Who's she?

—My friend from Naples.

—What about her?

—She asked her parents to do the same thing and they went for it.

—Mom would never go for it. This is her house, hers down

to the smallest detail. And as for Dad, it's proof that something came of all those years of work.

—But their lives are over.

—I doubt it. They could still go on for another twenty years.

—Exactly. And in twenty years I'll be sixty-five and you'll be seventy, assuming we get that far. What will I do, when I'm sixty-five, with half of this house? Think. Don't turn me into the heartless bitch as usual. They're two old people. What's the point of their living in a castle with a view of the Tiber?

He shakes his head, looking at me with sage disapproval. He wants me to feel that I'm in the wrong. He's done this ever since we were little. The money appeals to him, naturally. I see it in his face. But I know him, I see how he squirms inside. Ideally, he'd want me to do this all on my own—talk to our parents, convince them, sell the house, split the money between him and me, naturally in two equal parts—and meanwhile, I leave him the role of the doubtful son who raises ethical objections, who worries about Mom and Dad. Part of me knows that, if I want his consent, I shouldn't take him head-on. I have to put up with his scolding with my heart in my hands. But another part of me is getting antsy already. Like it or not, I have my scruples, too. I'm not made of stone. Which is why, if he keeps prodding me, I don't know where we'll end up. But he isn't just prodding me, he's wounding me.

—How would you react, he asks me, if, in thirty years your children did the same thing to you?

6.

I reply with vehemence. I've learned just one thing from our parents, I tell him: that you shouldn't have children. Then with false calm, choking on my words, I insist: You end up damaging your kids in any case, and so you have to expect them to damage you even more. I know he doesn't like extreme statements like this, but I use them on purpose. He's brought four children recklessly into the world. Let's see how he gets by.

He gets by in his usual way, praising himself. He's convinced, naturally, that the right road is the one he's been on: multiplying mothers, multiplying fatherhood, multiplying the nucleus of love and sex. And a confusion of roles. The end, in other words, of the traditional concept of the couple: no monogamy, various women, all of them loved, various children, all of them adored: When I take care of the kids—he tells me with his usual saccharine arrogance—I make sure they don't want for anything. I'm both father and mother to them.

I try not to reply. I give him time to boast about his grand views. But my brother gets under my skin, no matter how much I try not to let him. And so, at a certain point, I toss out the fact that he's never really escaped from the disaster that we were raised in, that he unloads the same heartache onto his children that our mother transferred to us: the man who becomes a woman, the woman who becomes a man, the father who becomes a mother, the mother who becomes a father. Domestic cross-dressing, verbal cosmetics, you're a terrorized little boy. And while I talk, the rage that usually stays put somewhere keeps rising in my chest. I hiss that I support the abolition of children, the abolition of pregnancy and childbirth, yes, ab-o-li-tion. I even want to erase the memory of reproduction by means of the female belly. Our genitals should serve only to piss and fuck. Not only that, I scream—I don't even know if fucking is all that it's cracked up to be. And we fight—Labes freaks out, he slips away, we overlap, sentence for sentence, word for word. How many clichés is he capable of unsheathing to defend himself? Pressing close to a loved one at night calms you down, love is better than faith in God, it's like a prayer in the face of the constant risk of death; having kids lowers anxiety, oh how sweet the joys of one's brood, how thrilling to see them grow: You realize you're a ring in an endless chain, those before you and those to come, it's the only way to feel immortal; et cetera et cetera et cetera.

I listen. He seems to be delivering a well-meaning sermon, but actually his goal is to make me feel bad. He wants me to envy him his happiness for all his offspring. He wants me to regret not having had children, he wants me to suffer. You— he emphasizes—don't have any and can't understand, that's why you're full of shit. It's true, I can't understand, I tell him, losing my calm for good. I can't understand your blind insemination, I can't understand all these trembling mares dripping bodily fluids, their ears pressed to their ticking biological clocks. Biological clock, what an inane term. I never heard any ticking. Time ran away, silently, and it's better that way. Imagine if I had a kid, screaming with pain. If I let myself be cut up under anesthesia and then woke up, disgusted with myself, depressed, overwhelmed by the terror of these little puppets you can't ignore. Right, you live for them. You've made them—cut and paste—and you have to hold on to them, whatever happens. You get offered a nice job abroad, or you need to work day and night for something you care about, or you want to give all the time you have to a man: but no, children stick around to remind you that you can't, there they are, they need you, little exasperating snakes with their clenched, ferocious writhing. Whatever you do to make them happy it's always too little. They want you for themselves, and they invent anything to put a wrench in the works. Not only are you not your own person—that old saying is bullshit, too—but you can't even try to belong fully to anyone else, by now you really only belong to them. And so, I scream, having kids means giving up yourself. Take a look at yourself, for once and for all, and see how you really live. Now you run to Provence, to Corinne's, to give her back the kids, then you'll go to Carla's little girl, then to Gina's boy. Oh, what a great dad, what a lover. But are you happy? And they, when you get there, when you leave, are they happy? I have a vague memory of when Dad came to see us on the weekends. I don't remember exact events but an unbearable feeling of unhappiness stuck with me—that's for certain—and it's never gone away. I wanted my father for myself. I wanted to take him away from you and Mom. But he wasn't any of ours, he was there and yet he wasn't. He'd given up me, you, Mom. And I quickly realized he'd done the right thing. Away, away, away. Our mother, to him, was the negation of the joy of living, and us too, you and me. Don't fool yourself, that's what we were, the negation, the negation. His real mistake was being unable to give us up for good. His mistake was that once you've taken action to hurt people profoundly, to kill or, in any case, permanently devastate other human beings, you can't go back. You have to accept the responsibility for the crime through and through. You can't commit a half-crime. But he's nothing, he's just a little man, numbed inside. He resisted as long as he felt he was in the right, as long as he felt he had others' approval. Then, as soon as everything started to settle and the approval ebbed, as soon as the fizz died down and he felt remorse, he caved. He came back and delivered himself to Mom's sadism. And she said to him: Let's see what your intentions are. I don't trust you, I'll never trust you, I won't ever believe that you came back for me and for the children; I won't believe you because I know it in my bones, in the deepest part of my being, the cost of a final choice like that. Which is why, every minute, every hour, I'll put you to the test. I'll put your patience, your faithfulness, to the test. I'll do it in front of the kids so that they see, so that they know the man you are. Say yes or no: Do you want to sacrifice your life to us the way I sacrifice mine to you? Are you prepared to put the three of us first all the time? To hell with loving each other, Sandro, to hell with reconstructing the family. Our parents destroyed us. They lodged themselves in our heads, and whatever we say or do, we keep obeying them.

At this point, given that I'm stupid, I can't help it and I burst into tears. That's right, I cry, I cry like any idiot, without knowing why. I'm enraged with myself for this fragility. My brother knows how to take advantage of it. But he doesn't. He seems shaken by my monologue, he tries to calm me down. So I tamp down my sobs, I dry my tears. My voice turns meek, I complain that no one loves me, not even Mom, not even Dad. They've never loved me, I say. And I'm pissed at the gratitude that children owe their parents, for the life they received. Gratitude? I laugh. I shout out: It's our parents who owe us a compensation. For the ways they've damaged our brains, our feelings. Don't you think? Then I blow my nose. I murmur, patting my hand on the couch, Labes, come here.

The cat surprises me: He leaps up and settles by my side.

7.

I'm tired. Crying has given way to a headache, I suffer from them like Dad. But the tears have also had a positive effect. I feel that the distance between me and Sandro has diminished, and if play my cards right, he'll be the one to bring up my proposal next. Caressing Labes, I decide to reveal a secret to my brother, something I discovered by chance a while back, when, for work, I was leafing through a Latin dictionary. I tell him what the name means; it means misfortune, it means ruin. He looks skeptical. He knows Dad's official version, that Labes is the beast of the house. To convince him, I go to the study, immediately trailed by the cat, and pull out the dictionary. Man, it's hot. When I'm back I sit down on the floor. I find the word, I underline it along with its definitions, then I nod to Sandro. I want him to say something about that wretched discovery. He joins me, unmotivated. Well, he says softly, why would he have done that? He doesn't say anything else, he seems distracted. I insist: What kind of man invents games like this for his own amusement? Is he depraved? Or just unhappy? Do you realize what it means to want to hear, continuously, through this house, a word that sums up how you feel inside, a word you chose, and that your family uses without knowing what it means? He smiles, faintly, I don't know if it's because he's siding with me, and he finally goes back to talking about selling the apartment.

—Where would they put all the stuff they have? he asks.

—They need to toss out more than half of it. We've moved so many times, but Mom never threw anything away, and she made you and me hold on to every little thing, too. You might need it, she'd say, you might need it if only to remember when you were little. Remember? Who wants to remember? I hate my room, it stresses me out just to be in it, all the crap you can think of is in there, from when I was born to when I finally escaped.

—Mine's the same.

—See? And if what I'm saying is true about our rooms, can you imagine what happens if we go through their stuff? For example: Did you know that Mom keeps all her shopping ledgers—bread, pasta, eggs, fruit—from the day she was married, 1962, till today? And Dad? He even hangs on to the junk he wrote when he was thirteen. Without factoring in the newspapers and magazines he published in, notes on the books he read, transcripts of his dreams, and so on. Fuck, he's hardly Dante Alighieri. He wrote some lame stuff for television, that's it. If anyone really cares about his thoughts—and I doubt it— you digitalize it and settle the matter.

—It's their way of leaving some trace.

—A trace of what?

—Of their lives.

—Do I leave a trace? Do you? This mad drive to conserve is Mom's thing, Dad couldn't give a shit.

He smiles, and I see, in his eyes, an unhappiness that, this time, looks genuine.

—You think so?

—Of course. If we convince them to sell, we give their lives a deep cleaning and do them both a favor.

—I don't think to.

—Why not?

—In this house there's visible order, but a disorder that's real.

—Explain what you mean.

—I won't explain anything to you, I'll show you.

He gets up, motioning for me to follow. Labes runs behind us. We go into Dad's study. Sandro points to the bookcase.

—Ever looked in that cube up there?

8.

I pretend that I'm enjoying myself, but actually, crying hasn't been a release. I feel a bitterness that's making me tense. If my brother abruptly takes off his mask and decides to show me how he's softened, it means I need to worry. I see him climb quickly up the ladder, and he comes back down with this blue cube, covered with dust. He wipes the dust off it with the sleeve of his shirt, and hands it to me.

—Do you remember it?

No, it's never intrigued me, nothing in this house has ever intrigued me. I detest its thousands of tacky things. I detest every room, every window, every balcony, also the glint of the river, the oppressive sky. Sandro, meanwhile, says that he remembers that cube from forever, that we already had it in the house when we lived in Naples. Look what a pretty color it is—he says softly—and how it's polished: To him it's the most amazing geometric shape there is. When for some reason our parents were out—he tells me—I used to rummage everywhere. That was how he once discovered condoms in our father's bedside table and vaginal cream in the one on our mother's side. Oh, gross, I blurt out, but then I'm ashamed: I'm forty-five years old, I've been with an impressive number of men and women, and yet I still feel disgusted thinking of my parents having sex? Sandro looks, unsure, at my hands. He says: Enough, you're trembling. I'm surprised by his tone, genuinely delicate. He takes back the cube and he's already clambering with ease up the ladder to put it back in its place. I get angry. I say, don't be an idiot, come back down, what do you want me to see? He stops up there, wavering. It's a box—then he says—you open it by pressing against this side. And he presses, and indeed the box opens. He shakes it and causes a certain number of Polaroids fall out.

I kneel down to collect them. They show a person both he and I know very well. It's exactly the way we know her, with this happy face. She entered our consciousness one morning when we'd stopped—me, him, and Mom—on a quiet street in Rome. We'd come from Naples for this purpose. We felt dark dread inside, she was the one we were waiting for. Mom explained it to us: she said, let's wait for her to come through that door with Dad. And in fact, when our father and this girl stepped out—they were so beautiful together, they sparkled— Mom told us: There, see how happy Dad is? That's Lidia, the woman he left us for. Lidia: Even now the name feels like an animal's bite. When Mom pronounced it her desperation became ours, the three of us inhabiting a single body. But on that occasion, as I watched that woman carefully, the single organism I belonged to broke apart. I thought: How pretty she is, how cheerful. When I grow up I want to be just like her. But this thought made me feel immediately guilty. I still feel guilty,

I've felt guilty all my life. I realized I didn't want to resemble my mother anymore, and that I was thus betraying her. Had I the courage I would have shouted, Dad, Lidia, I want to go for a walk with you. I don't want to stay with Mom, she scares me. Instead, now, in this precise moment, I feel incredibly sorry for my mother, and also for myself. Lidia is naked, she's glowing. The two of us aren't like her, we never were. The secret presence of these pictures proves it. My dad never left Lidia, and how could he: He kept her hidden in his mind and in our house his whole life. While we were the ones, even though he came back, that he left. And now that I'm much older than the Lidia in these photos, also older than my mother in that time of unbearable pain, seeing her makes me feel even more humiliated.

—How long have you known about these? I ask my brother, who's come down from the ladder.

—About thirty years.

—And why didn't you ever show them to our mother?

—I don't know.

—And to me?

He shrugs. It means he can no longer be bothered trying to convince me of his good intentions. I whine:

—You're so good. You're all so good with women. You have three big goals in life: fuck us, protect us, screw us up.

9.

Sandro shakes his head, saying something about the state of my health. I tell him I'm fine, rather, that I feel great. It's also great that I told him about Labes's name, and that he told me the story about the blue cube. Now we know a little more about our father. What a man, never protests, always yes, yes. He was and remains Mom's slave. I hated so much that she ruled with an iron rod, and that he let himself be tortured, never rebelling. And I hated him so much for never lifting a finger to protect us from her. Dad, I need this. Ask Mom. She says no. Well then, no.

I examine the photos, and one by one I let them fall to the floor.

—What else do you know that I don't? I ask my brother.

Sandro patiently gathers up the photos.

—I don't know anything else about Dad, but you just need to poke around to learn more.

—And about Mom?

He admits reluctantly to having various suspicions. He's convinced that our mother had lovers. Proof, I said, not speculation. You have to want to find the proof, he replies. And he confesses that for years he thought that she'd had an affair with Nadar. Nadar? I exclaim, laughing: I don't even want to think about it, Mom with that eyesore, Nadar, what a ridiculous name. Sandro insists. Maybe it happened in 1985, you were sixteen and I was twenty. I ask: And Mom? I never knew how to do math in my head. He answers: Forty-seven, two years less than I am today, two more than you. And Nadar? No idea, sixty-two? Oh my God, I exclaim, forty-seven and sixty-two. Then I laugh again and shake my head, incredulous: How disgusting, I don't believe it.

But my brother believes it, I realize he's always believed it. Looking around, he says: Something emerges sooner or later. If it's not Nadar it's someone else, you just need to check inside a flower vase or in the pages of a book or on the computer. He lists a number of possible objects. I look at them for the first time, curious. I feel my mother and father. I feel them in the silent rooms, together and apart. Sandro says: They hid from each other, but not without the threat of discovering each other at any moment. At this point, for no apparent reason, his eyes start to shine. He's one of those men who flaunt knowing how to cry. He reads a novel, you ask him how it is, and he says: I cried. He sees a film, ditto. Now he bursts into tears and cries more than I cried a little while ago. He always tends to overdo it. To calm him I hug him and stay close, while Labes mews, disoriented. Maybe I was unfair to Sandro. He was the older one, he remembered more. Our parents' troubles fell onto him first and then—maybe they really were filtered by his zeal to protect—onto me. I say, come on, enough, let's have little fun, let's throw a little light on things.

10.

They were carefree hours, perhaps the most lighthearted ever spent in this house. We rummaged everywhere, room after room. In the beginning we limited ourselves to upending our parents' order, trailed cheerfully by the cat. Then we got our hands dirty and went on to dismantle everything. It was getting hotter, I was sweaty, and before long I got tired. I told Sandro: That's enough. But he kept going, with increasing fervor. So I brought a chair onto the balcony off the living room, and I was pleased to see that the cat was taking refuge beside me. I gathered him into my arms, talking to him for a while. My mind had cleared, even my fixation with convincing our parents to sell the apartment had vanished. What an insane idea. Sandro reappeared, he'd taken his shirt off. Just like Dad, I thought. He looked at me, laughing:

—Well?

—I've had my fill.

—Should we go?

—Yes. Labes wants to come with me.

He frowned.

—No, that's going too far.

—Actually, yes, I'm taking him away with me.

—Leave Mom a note.

—No.

—Then call her as soon as she's back.

—What for?

—She'll suffer.

—The cat won't. See how happy he is?

Domenico Starnone is an Italian writer, screenwriter and journalist. He was born in Naples and lives in Rome. He is the author of thirteen works of fiction, including *First Execution* (Europa 2009) and *Via Gemito*, winner of Italy's most prestigious literary prize, the Strega.